PRAISE FOR JAMES SCOTT BELL

James Scott Bell has produced gold in the Mike Romeo series, about a one-time cage fighter and certified genius on a quest for virtue. I want to be Mike Romeo when I get younger. *Romeo's Rage* was thrilling and moving. Highly recommended.

— **LARS WALKER, BRANDYWINE BOOKS**

A master of the cliffhanger, creating scene after scene of mounting suspense and revelation . . . Heart-whamming.

— **PUBLISHERS WEEKLY**

A master of suspense.

— **LIBRARY JOURNAL**

One of the best writers out there, bar none.

— **IN THE LIBRARY REVIEW**

There'll be no sleeping till after the story is over.

— **JOHN GILSTRAP**, NYT BESTSELLING AUTHOR

D1616937

James Scott Bell's series is as sharp as a switchblade.

— **MEG GARDINER**, EDGAR AWARD
WINNING AUTHOR

One of the top authors in the crowded suspense genre.

— **SHELDON SIEGEL**, NYT BESTSELLING
AUTHOR

ROMEO'S FIRE

JAMES SCOTT BELL

Compendium Press

Compendium Press
Woodland Hills, CA

ISBN: 978-0-910355-61-2

Then the fire of the Lord fell, and consumed the burnt sacrifice, and the wood, and the stones, and the dust, and licked up the water that was in the trench.

— 1 KINGS 18:38

I've seen fire and I've seen rain.

— JAMES TAYLOR

ROMEO'S FIRE

"Why aren't you married?"

It was one o'clock in the afternoon and I was washing Mrs. Edna Morgenstern's windows. Mrs. Morgenstern is an octogenarian widow who lives next door to Ira Rosen in the Los Feliz district of Los Angeles. Whenever I'm at Ira's and she spots me, Mrs. Morgenstern will ask—demand—that I assist her in some task around her house. Ira encourages me in this. He says it keeps me human and humble—two things I am rarely accused of.

I'd just put the finishing touch on her front room window, using a mixture of water and vinegar. It counterbalanced the smell of Mrs. Morgenstern's egg salad, which she was threatening to serve me for lunch.

"A man your age should be married," Mrs. Morgenstern said. She wore a flower-patterned housedress and an expression that would wither a vine. "You're young and vigorous. You should have children. That means you should take a wife. What's wrong with you?"

That list was too long to go into, so I said, "I'm waiting for a woman like you, Mrs. Morgenstern."

"You're a scamp," she said. "I'll just bet you run around with a lot of girls."

"Haven't got the money," I said.

"Nonsense! When I was your age we used to go to the skating rink, or bowling, or the arcade. We didn't have to be fancy-schmancy."

"The good old days," I said.

"I don't understand young people," she said.

I stood back from the window. "Clear as crystal."

"Don't change the subject."

"There's a subject?" I said.

"Getting married! Sit down."

"I really have to get—"

"Down!"

Keeping on the good side of Edna Morgenstern, I've discovered, makes life more pleasant for Ira. I didn't want his boat rocked. He has enough trouble looking out for my boat, which needs the constant scraping of barnacles and is kept in dry dock whenever possible. I sat on her sofa, which Mrs. Morgenstern calls a Davenport.

"I met Samuel in 1958," she said. "That was a good year, before all the hippies and whatnot, with their long hair and those smells! It was at a wedding we met, for Mildred Klump, my best high school friend. Sammy was at another table and he made eyes at me. And let me tell you, he knew how to make eyes. You could make eyes if you wanted to."

I cleared my throat.

"Fifty-two years we were married," Mrs. Morgenstern said. "All because he made eyes. You do the same, young man. Find yourself a girl and make eyes at her. Then get married. No hanky-panky before that."

She gave me a serious stare.

"I really must be going now, Mrs. Morgenstern," I said, standing and moving sideways toward the front door.

"You haven't had your lunch yet!"

"I think I hear Ira calling me," I said.

"I didn't hear anything," she said.

"There it is again." I opened the door.

"Do come back soon," Mrs. Morgenstern said. "I so enjoy our little chats!"

"Whew," I said as I walked into Ira's home and law office. He is a rabbi, lawyer, former Mossad agent, my employer, my conscience, and the man who has provided me a place to live in Paradise Cove. In other words, I'd be lost without him.

"All through with Mrs. Morgenstern?" Ira asked. He was at his desk in the front room.

"She's not all through with me, that's for sure," I said.

"Ah, but your soul shall be made fat."

"Excuse me?"

"Proverbs, chapter eleven, verse twenty-five. It means he who serves another, in the true spirit of charity, shall not fail to receive God's blessing, a hundred fold."

"Let's eat," I said.

Ira turned his wheelchair to face me. "We have a client."

"Oh?"

"Judge Fraser called me." Ira is on a list of attorneys who take assigned cases when there's a conflict within the Public Defender's office.

"A young man accused of second-degree murder," Ira said. "He's being held downtown. We can go meet with him now, then repair to Langer's for a Number 19."

Langer's is the legendary deli across from MacArthur Park, serving the best hot pastrami

sandwich in the country, no matter what New Yorkers say. The Number 19 is pastrami, Swiss cheese and coleslaw with

Russian dressing, all on their site-made rye bread with just the right crust crunch. If Beethoven had designed a sandwich, this would be it.

"Your plan meets with my approval," I said.

H alf an hour later we were in the attorney room at the jail. A deputy sheriff marched in with a sallow youth in his early twenties. He was skinny, with long, stringy hair, and his blue jumpsuit hung loosely over his bony frame. He had large doe eyes and a face with a goofy look that almost made you want to laugh.

The deputy sat him across from us and stepped out of the room.

"Coby Keaton?" Ira said.

He nodded. "Are you my lawyer?"

"I am. Ira Rosen. And this is my investigator, Mike Romeo."

Coby Keaton looked at me. "You're a big guy. Now that's funny."

"Funny?" I said.

"Look at me," Coby said. "If I stand sideways and stick out my tongue, I look like a zipper."

I stared at him.

"That's funny, isn't it?" Coby said.

"You're being charged with second-degree murder," Ira said.

"What's that mean, exactly?" Coby said.

"That you acted without premeditation, but also without lawful excuse or justification."

Any mirth that had been on his face disappeared. He closed his eyes. "That stinks, man, that really sucks. That's not the way it went down, no way."

Ira said, "Let's just take this one step at a time. You tell us what happened. Give me your story, okay?"

"Okay. I—"

"Just one thing before you do, Coby," Ira said. "We can't help you if you lie to us. You can trust us. You understand?"

"Okay."

"I mean really understand," Ira said.

Coby's eyes widened. "Yes."

"By the way, did you make any statement to the police?"

"Started to," Coby said. "But then I remembered the cop shows. I asked them to get me a lawyer."

"Good," Ira said. "From now on you talk only to me or Mike, got it?"

He nodded.

"Just take us through it," Ira said. "Tell us how you got here."

"To L.A. you mean?" Coby said.

"Sure," Ira said. "Start there."

C oby Keaton was twenty-four and had been homeless for over two years. He'd left his sister's house in Vegas and moved to L.A. hoping to make it as a comedian. He stayed with a high school friend, Brad Skinner, for a few weeks, sleeping on his couch while he hit the bricks looking for his big break. All he needed was one good night at an open mic, with just the right producer or agent in the audience.

He got turned down at The Laugh Factory. They told him to get some gigs under his belt somewhere else because you don't start at the top, kid. He finally found a new club in NoHo that gave him a spot in an eleven o'clock roundhouse—ten new comedians getting five minutes each at the microphone. Coby followed a guy who absolutely killed. While Coby's jokes didn't fall flat, they didn't light any fires, either.

Same thing happened a week later. Then the club told him to try another venue.

"I was getting desperate," Coby said. "I used the last of my money on weed. Brad's girlfriend got tired of seeing me baked on their couch all the time, and Brad told me I'd have to go. I couldn't really blame him. I was a mess."

"Where did you go?" Ira said.

Where he went was to his car, where he lived for almost a year. The only good thing at that time was that Covid hit and the state was handing out other people's money, which kept Coby afloat while he honed his act and kept himself in ganja.

Then the money stopped. And his car was stolen.

Coby started living on the street. Which meant finding a space you could call your own, as long as you could hang onto it. And stay alive.

"I found a nook by the library parking entrance," he said. "I got some sleep the first night. The second night four guys beat me up. They smelled like the gutter after it rains. I almost died. When I came to, I was staring into a hairy face."

The face belonged to someone calling himself Zon. He had a tamarindo drink from Pinches Tacos and shared it with Coby, then sat with him because Coby didn't feel safe anymore.

It was Zon who suggested they share a tent on the bridge over the 101 Freeway.

"About a week later," Coby said, "Zon was gone somewhere and a hype beat me up and took all my panhandling money. That was it. I was gonna jump onto the freeway. I was done. But I kept thinking about my sister. She's the one person in my stinking life who believes in me, told me I could make it. I didn't want to hurt her. So I went out panhandling and got some money, and went to a pawn shop on Broadway and bought a knife. Zon thought it was a good idea. Some joke."

"What kind of knife was it?" Ira said.

"A switchblade," Coby said.

"Go on."

"So two days ago I wake up in the tent, it's the afternoon. Zon isn't there. So I take my sign to the corner of First and Alameda, and hold it up. My sign says *Hungry comedian. Will make you laugh for money.*"

He made seven dollars and a handful of change in an hour and a half. A big part of that was a fiver he got from a guy in sunglasses driving a convertible Beamer. "Hey," the guy had shouted. "Make me laugh."

Coby was prepped. "I gave a smartphone to my dumb cousin. Now he's average."

The sunglasses guy smiled. "Not bad, kid." He held out the Abe Lincoln. "Here you go."

"Man," Coby said to us in the attorney room, "if that guy was only a club owner."

He then headed to the Subway shop on 2nd and ordered a footlong meatball sandwich and wolfed it down, chased by a large Mountain Dew.

"The Dew is my only drug of choice," Coby said. "Besides weed. I know enough not to get hooked on meth, like Zon was. As I was heading back to the bridge, I saw a wild man in the middle of the intersection of Los Angeles and Third, screaming at cars. He was completely naked. It was Zon. Cars honked, Zon waved his arms. So I ran over and heard Zon screaming, Lucifer is coming!"

"Lucifer?" Ira said.

"Yeah," Coby said. "Lucifer is coming. He was meth crazy. I shouted at him, 'Zon, man, get outta the street!' He looked me. Man, there was fire in his eyes. He charged at me. I couldn't move. He grabbed my throat. He was gonna kill me. He said it again, 'Lucifer is coming,' and sprayed spit on me. I had to do something. I got my knife and . . . stabbed him. He wouldn't let go. I was losing air. I stabbed him again. Blood was coming out . . . "

He stopped. He was having trouble breathing.

"Easy now," Ira said. "What happened next?"

"We fell down on the sidewalk. Zon flopped around like a fish. He let go of my throat. I put my hands on his stomach where I stabbed him. His blood was so hot! I kept pressing and pressing until Zon stopped moving. That was that."

"You were in fear for your life," Ira said.

"Yeah," Coby said.

"Under those facts, what you did was self-defense," Ira said. "The problem is the knife. In California, you can legally purchase, own, transport, and carry any knife that is not restricted under the law. But a switchblade with a blade longer than two inches is illegal. It shouldn't have been available at the pawn shop. The prosecution may try to say you had it because you had intent to kill."

"But I didn't!" Coby said.

"Do you know if there were witnesses to Zon's attack on you?"

"There were people around, in cars, too," Coby said. "But I don't know what they saw."

"We'll find out," Ira said. "There may be camera footage. Next, let's see about getting you out of here. Do you have any place you can stay, other than the street?"

Coby shook his head. Then, "Wait, maybe Sonhouse."

"Sonhouse Rescue Mission," Ira said.

"Yeah. Zon went there once. They take you in and help you stay clean, if you follow the rules."

"Can you follow the rules?" Ira said.

"Oh yeah," Coby said.

"Your arraignment is coming up," Ira said. "I'll see about getting you into Sonhouse in lieu of bail."

"I thought there wasn't bail anymore," Coby said.

"Only for non-violent offenses," Ira said.

Coby took a deep breath. "Am I gonna go to prison?"

"Not on our watch," Ira said.

"Good," Coby said. Then he smiled. "I heard about a man with a stutter who died in prison."

Ira and I just looked at him.

"He never got to finish his sentence," Coby said. "That's funny, right?"

A nd so we went to Langer's. Got a booth by the window looking out at Alvarado and the corner of MacArthur Park. A tent city was across the street, only in this city, stuffed shopping carts made fences, and sprawled bodies were the shrubs. A woman on wobbly legs walked into the intersection holding a little boy's hand. The boy had on shorts and shoes, but no shirt. He was sucking his thumb.

"The city of dreams," I said.

"Entropy," Ira said.

"How's that?"

"Everything runs down unless energy is infused," Ira said. "The energy of Los Angeles used to be self-reliance, ambition, and private enterprise. Crime and taxes have drained that. And so you see." He motioned with his hand at the street scene.

"It's not coming back, is it?" I said.

"Not without spiritual renewal, repentance, and will," Ira said. "I don't see much of that in City Hall or Sacramento."

"History is not exactly replete with repentance," I said.

"In the time of the Judges, the people were conquered and had to cry out to the Lord before he sent them a deliverer."

"Like Samson," I said.

"Very good," Ira said.

"He was my man. Killed a thousand Philistines with the jawbone of a lawyer."

"Watch it," Ira said.

Our pastrami sandwiches came. For this I require a squeeze

bottle of brown mustard. I dollop a bit before each bite, otherwise I can't get the balance right.

"So you don't think the kid'll do time?" I asked.

"He shouldn't," Ira said. "But the DA's office is, shall we say, erratic."

"That's a kind word for it," I said.

"I'm feeling charitable today."

"I'm not," I said, looking out the window again. I was thinking of the little boy sucking his thumb. But he was nowhere to be seen.

B ack at Ira's we discussed a few strategies. I said I'd go Sonhouse and prep them to take in Coby. Around two I got in my classic Mustang, Spinoza, and drove home to Paradise Cove.

The Cove is a little slice of heaven on the Pacific Ocean. I live in Ira's mobile unit there. We're a little community, a mix of second homes for A-listers up on the bluffs, and retirees who bought in long ago in the flats. And a few who are legacies living off the largesse of wealthy parents.

One of the latter was sitting on my porch.

Carter "C Dog" Weeks is a rocker who used to con the government out of food stamp money in order to buy weed and snacks for his band Unopened Cheese. Lately, with a little encouragement from me, he's been making strides in the right direction.

He stood and said, "Look!"

He held up his left hand. His middle finger was puffy and red, like a stuffed sausage.

"I can't play," he said in a plaintive wail. "It hurts!"

"What happened?"

"I don't know! I whacked it a couple of nights ago at a gig, and today it looks like this. What do I do?"

"You get it looked at," I said. "Come on."

I put him in Spinoza and drove him to Artra Murray's medical clinic on PCH. Artra is a saint, former head of surgery at Johns Hopkins, now dedicated to helping the cashless flotsam and jetsam of current society.

Her young receptionist, Connie, smiled as we walked in. "Hello there, Mike!"

"Connie. Young C Dog here has a finger issue." I waved him up to the desk and had him show it to her.

"Oh my," Connie said. "Have a seat. I'll let Dr. Murray know you're here."

We sat. C Dog looked at his hand as if it were a foreign thing. "I'm scared, Mike. What if I can't play anymore?"

"It's one finger," I said. "Artra will know how to fix it."

"I hope so," C Dog said. "It'd kill me if I couldn't play."

"It wouldn't kill you," I said. "Besides, that which does not kill you makes you stronger."

"Huh?"

I held up my left hand. "Remember my little finger?"

"Oh, yeah. Guy cut it off with a knife."

"And I took it to a nearby hospital and they sewed it back on. It's not the same, but it's mostly workable."

"What if they cut off my finger?" C Dog said.

"You're a glass half empty kind of fellow," I said.

"Huh?"

"Ever heard of Django Reinhardt?"

"Who?"

"Greatest jazz guitarist of all time. When he was younger than you he got burned badly in a fire, including the ring finger and pinkie of his left hand. The docs said he'd never play guitar again. So what did he do? Figured out a new way to play using his index and middle fingers. And became a legend."

C Dog thought about it.

"You can be scared a little," I said. "But not too much, okay?"

"K, Mike."

Connie showed us to a little room. There was a chart on the wall showing the inner workings of the human body. She took C Dog's temp. It was a little over 100.

Artra came in wearing a white smock. "Hello, Carter, Mike. What have we got?"

C Dog held out his hand. Artra took him by the wrist and looked it over.

"That's some infection," she said. "We need to do a little draining."

"A little what?" C Dog said.

"Take out the bad stuff that's in there," Artra said. "We don't want this spreading."

C Dog looked at me as if this was the worst news in the world.

"You just sit here while we get ready," Artra said. Connie started gathering some items.

"And how are you, Mr. Romeo?" Artra said.

"Better than most, not as good as some," I said.

"A good place to be," she said.

Connie wheeled a medical tray over.

Artra said, "We're going to give you a shot of lidocaine. It's going to hurt, but this will be the worst part, okay?"

"Oh man," C Dog said.

Connie gently put C's hand on the tray. Artra sanitized his finger with a wipe, then gave it the needle.

C Dog winced, but didn't cry out. I was proud.

"We'll let it sit a minute," she said. "Then we'll drain. You won't feel a thing."

"I'm for that," C Dog said.

"So how's the music going?" Artra said.

"Okay, I guess," C Dog said.

"Ever play any Creedence? Doobie Brothers?"

"Just our own stuff."

"More's the pity," Artra said. "What's the name of your band again?"

"Grated Cheese," I said.

"*Unopened* Cheese," C Dog said.

"I saw Elton John in concert twice," Artra said. "Now that was a show."

"I saw Crudd in concert," I said.

"Crud?" C Dog said.

"With two d's," I said. "They were friends with the promoter I was fighting for in Knoxville."

"What kind of music did they play?" C Dog said.

"Did I mention music?" I said. "They made some loud noises. The extra d was for dreadful."

C Dog smiled and shook his head, which is when Artra stuck a needle on top of C Dog's infected digit. A few drops of cloudy, purplish blood went into the attached vial.

"Hmm," Artra said.

"What's that mean?" C Dog said.

"It's better than oops," I said.

"Need to find a better spot," Artra said. She turned C's hand over and repeated the procedure. This time the fluid flowed.

"There's the money," Artra said.

"What's that mean?" C Dog said.

"It means you're going to be fine, Carter," Artra said. "But it will take time to heal."

"Will I be able to play the guitar?" C Dog said.

"Of course," Artra said.

"That's funny," I said. "He could never play it before."

"What!" C Dog said.

"It's an old joke, Carter," Artra said. "And it was funny the first hundred times I heard it."

W hen it was all over, C Dog had a bandaged finger and we were on our way to a pharmacy to pick up antibiotics. After that we came back to my place. C Dog didn't want to leave. He asked me for a beer.

"Not while you're on the antibios," I said.

"What?"

"That's right. No booze."

"Come on!"

I got him a Coke instead, and broke out the chess board.

"It's time you learned," I said. "It'll be good for your brain."

"You always make my brain hurt," C Dog said.

"No pain, no gain."

I laid out the board and began explaining the way the pieces moved. C was confused about the knight, but he kept with it. Which was another major step for him.

Then I showed him a basic opening with White. "Always move the king's pawn first," I said. "That'll make things simpler."

I walked him through a few opening moves. "The idea in the opening is to develop your pieces, and aim for control of the center squares."

"You're good at everything, aren't you?"

"I'm not good at waiting," I said. "I'm a fugitive and a vagabond in the earth."

"A what?"

"It's a biblical reference," I said. "Have you heard about Cain and Abel?"

"I think so. Brothers, right?"

"Cain slew Abel. And God told Cain his brother's blood was calling out from the earth."

"Whoa."

"And Cain was cursed. The earth would no longer yield crops for him. He had to wander the earth, wondering somebody might kill him, too."

"That's messed up," C Dog said. "You saying you're cursed, Mike?"

"I do wonder sometimes about getting whacked," I said. "It's an occupational hazard."

"Why do you do it, then? Why don't you do something else?"

"Like what?"

He shrugged. "You like flowers. You could be one of those flower grower guys."

"You mean a horticulturist?"

"Is that what I mean?"

"I think so."

"Okay. So why not?"

"I'll give it some thought," I said.

"Will you do that, Mike?"

"Do what?"

"Give it some thought? Seriously?"

"What's up, C?"

He lowered his head, looked at the floor. "I don't want you to die, man. I got to have you around."

I put my hand on his shoulder. "Don't worry about it. I'm gonna be around for a long time."

"How do you know?" He looked up. He had tears in his eyes.

"Hey, pal," I said. "None of that."

"But you never know, right? I mean, you don't, right?"

"True enough, C. But you can't walk around with a giant question mark burning in your chest. You have to take life as it comes and make your best move." I tapped the chess board. "Which is what chess is about, too. Your move."

Wednesday morning I drove downtown to Sonhouse Rescue Mission. It's a few blocks from the middle of Skid Row in a building that formerly housed the Department of Water and Power. Ira had called ahead to set up a meeting with the Reverend Tatum Walker, who ran the place.

He met me at the reception desk. He was a barrel-chested man in his late forties with a ready smile and a strong handshake.

"Welcome," he said.

"Thanks for seeing me," I said.

"I know Ira Rosen's reputation. You must be a good man to be working for him."

"He's a good man for letting me," I said.

"You have a client to divert here?"

"That's right."

"Let me give you the cook's tour, even though I don't cook."

"That name comes from Thomas Cook," I said.

"How's that?"

"He was a British missionary. He organized quick tours to temperance meetings by train."

"No way! That makes it even better, 'cause of what we do here. How'd you know that?"

"I crack a book every now and then," I said.

"We're gonna get along fine, my brother."

He took me around the first floor of the facility which included a day room and dining hall, with several men engaged in cleaning and arranging chairs.

Then we went into a chapel. It had rows of chairs and a simple, wooden pulpit at the front. "The gospel is the cornerstone of everything we do," Walker said. "Chapel attendance is mandatory. Men's discipleship group is voluntary. There's a women's Bible study, too. Mostly, everybody on staff wants to be Jesus to anybody who comes through our doors."

"Anybody?" I said.

"Anybody. All they have to do is commit to obeying the rules. If they can't, we refer them elsewhere."

We ended the tour in his modest office off the front corridor. Tatum Walker's desk was neat and orderly, but his chair squeaked when he sat down. I sat in one of the chairs in front of the desk.

"Now, tell me about this client of yours," Walker said.

I gave him the rundown on Coby Keaton. Walker listened, nodding every now and then.

When I finished he said, "That's a big ask."

"I know it is," I said.

"But the Lord specializes in big asks," he said. "Because it's Ira Rosen, I'll make this a provisional yes. You can tell that to the court."

"Appreciate it," I said.

"Zon came through here a couple of times," Walker said. "He's another victim. I'm not talking about the way he was killed."

"How so?"

"He was a full-on meth head. Because of city policy."

"What policy is that?" I said.

"It's called Housing First. Sounds so nice, doesn't it? I mean, what do the homeless need most but a home? But it only makes the situation worse, 'cause a roof's all they offer. That doesn't make the situation any better, because it doesn't get at the root. And there's no requirement of better behavior, like we have. Know why? I'll tell you. I'll tell you…oh man, listen to me. Getting heated."

"It's okay," I said. "I've been known to get heated myself. Keep going."

"Well, it's like this. If you take federal funds for homeless relief, you can't require any conditions in return for housing assistance. None. So what happens in these housing units? Free flow of hard drugs. And then the city hands out needles and meth pipes, thinking at least we'll make things safer. Got that? Safer drug use. Then they say they got Naloxone for overdoses. But guess what? Down here they got meth mixed with fentanyl and horse tranquilizer. Naloxone doesn't work on horse tranq. You seen what people do on meth?"

"I have," I said.

"Crazy town, man. Take off their clothes, run through the streets, screaming, breaking windows on cars, buildings, getting cut up. But it ain't just crazy. It's demonic." He paused and leaned forward. "I mean that literally."

"Literal demons?"

"You don't believe?"

"It wouldn't surprise me," I said.

"People think they're so enlightened. Like there's no spirit world. You know what the Bible says about that?"

"Tell me," I said.

"Says we don't wrestle with flesh and blood, but against principalities and powers and rulers of this dark world, against spiritual wickedness in high places. You look at what's going on in the world right now, and you can't explain the hate and the wickedness without reference to Satan and demons."

"Speaking of which," I said, "did Zon ever say anything about Lucifer?"

Walker thought a moment. "Not that I remember."

"Because our client says he told him Lucifer is coming, Lucifer is coming."

"I got news for you," Walker said. "Lucifer's already here.

And he's not alone. You know about the ancient Canaanite gods?"

"Some. My mother taught theology at Yale."

"No kidding," Walker said. Then added with a wry smile, "They got theology at Yale?"

"She was a light in the darkness," I said.

"Was?"

"She's dead."

"I'm sorry," Walker said.

I said nothing.

"Maybe Zon heard one of my sermons on Revelation," Walker said.

"What would he have heard?"

Walker leaned back in his chair. "Mr. Romeo, I believe we are smack dab in the middle of Revelation, chapter twenty. It's the period called the unloosing of Satan. It's a time of unprecedented wickedness, right before the return of Christ. The Canaanite gods never went away, but were bound. Now they are unbound. Baal, Molech. You know about Molech?"

"Child sacrifice," I said.

Walker nodded. "In Leviticus it says, And thou shalt not let any of thy seed pass through the fire to Molech. They would sacrifice the first born child in fire to please this demon god. What do we call it today when pre-born children are sacrificed? Health care. The rest of the verse in Leviticus is, neither shalt thou profane the name of thy God. I am the Lord."

"Serious," I said.

"Got that right," Walker said. "You know, I used to argue with atheists by trying to prove the existence of God. But the atheist mind is so closed that I've found it more effective to get to God through the back door."

"Back door?"

"Prove the existence of Satan," he said. "You cannot look at the hate, the violence, the utter unspeakable wickedness and not conclude that an evil and powerful presence is at work, blinding the mind and searing the conscience. Satan was held back from full power since the crucifixion of Christ. Now the chain has been removed. Satan is at full strength, with his army. But this is for a little season. It will seem as if this army surrounds the camp of the saints, ready to deliver a death blow. But that is when fire will come down from heaven and destroy them. Then, with the sound of the trumpet and the voice of the archangel, Jesus Christ will return with the host of heaven for Satan's final doom. It cannot come soon enough."

His eyes were on fire, like an Old Testament prophet. Then they cooled. "Sorry, got a little carried away."

"I don't mind," I said. "I like it when ideas are expressed with conviction."

"I don't know if I've helped at all with your question about Zon."

"I'll take what I can," I said.

"You ought to talk to Tommy," Walker said. "He's one of our counselors. Zon was assigned to him."

"Is he around?"

"Let me check." He picked up his phone. "And anytime you want to talk about spiritual warfare, I'm your man."

"I'll remember that," I said.

The office next to Walker's was similar in design, but more stuffed with haphazard papers on the desk and stacks of files on the floor. There was a filing cabinet next to the door, which I presumed to be so full there wasn't room for the others.

At the desk was a man who was almost the exact opposite of Tatum Walker. Short, wide, bald, wearing glasses.

"Tommy, this is Mike Romeo," Walker said.

Thompson stood, smiled, and reached out his hand. We shook.

"He's got some questions about Zon," Walker said.

"Oh," Thompson said. "Sure."

"I'll leave you to it." Walker slapped me on the shoulder and left the office.

Thompson gestured to a chair and I sat.

"Sorry for the mess," Thompson said.

"Must be a tough gig," I said.

"Which makes it so satisfying," Thompson said. "It saved my life."

"Oh?"

"Long story, but that's not why you're here."

"I've got nothing but time," I said.

"It's an old story," he said. "It's kind of a cliché, really. I was a high school teacher, ten years, loved it. But man, between the union and administration, and parents who complain because little Susie didn't get an A plus and you're ruining her life because she won't get into Harvard. And all they give you is a couple two-hour shifts each week to prep for classes, and then they schedule meetings at those same times and expect you to go on like everything's no problem. It's just insane."

"And typical."

"Yeah. And then I have to pick up extra income just to live in this town, with a wife and son. A colleague introduces me to meth. Says a little bit will help me cope, give me energy. And he was right about that. At first. You know the rest. Taking more and more, caught and confronted by a student in the faculty bathroom. The faculty bathroom! Anyway, I lost my job, my wife, my son. And almost my life. That's when Tatum Walker found me."

"Found you?"

"Right outside these walls. That was a little over two years ago."

"You seem like the right man for the job."

"God put me here," Thompson said. "I'll spend the rest of my life serving him. Now, you wanted to know about Zon?"

"What was his full name?" I said.

"He never used but the one name."

"He ever talk to you about Lucifer?"

"Not that I recall," Thompson said.

"It was something he was shouting when the killing happened. Lucifer is coming, he kept saying."

"Interesting," Thompson said.

"Why interesting?" I said.

"Oh, just because of what's going on outside these doors."

"Reverend Walker was filling me in," I said. "You think that's what was in Zon's mind, such as it was?"

"His mind was fried," Thompson said. "Probably on meth, though heroin is not out of the question. It's been making a comeback, sad to say." He paused. "Interesting that he used the name Lucifer."

"How so?"

"Lucifer means light bearer. Paul tells us in Second Corinthians that Satan masquerades as an angel of light. That's what people don't get. They think the devil has horns and a tail. In fact, his beauty would inspire awe."

"All right," I said. "If anything else occurs to you—"

"Hold on a sec," he said. "One of our volunteers spent a good deal of time with him." Thompson took up his phone and thumbed a text.

. . .

A few minutes later a young man, mid-twenties, came into the office. He was around six feet, on the thin side, dressed in slacks and a sweater, with brown hair and intelligent eyes.

"This is Nathan White," Thompson said. "Nathan, this is Mike Romeo."

I shook his hand.

"You spent some time with Zon in Bible study, didn't you?" Thompson said.

"I did, yes," Nathan White said.

"What do you know about him?" I said.

"That he was from San Diego," Nathan White said. "He'd been on the street for three or four years. And he was intensely interested in the Bible."

"Did he ever talk to you about Lucifer?" I said.

He thought about it. "No. Why do you ask?"

"It was something he was shouting before he died," I said.

"Oh man," Nathan White said.

"Nathan," Thompson said, "if anything else occurs to you, let me know, will you?"

"Sure thing," he said. "Nice to meet you, Mr. Romeo."

"Ditto," I said.

He left the office.

"I'll help you in any way I can," Thompson said. "Just let me know."

"Thanks." I stood to go.

"God be with you, Mr. Romeo," he said.

"I'm all for that," I said.

I left my car parked at Sonhouse and walked a few blocks to Grand Central Market. The Market has been around over a hundred years. It takes up the entire ground floor of the Beaux-

Arts-style Homer Laughlin Building. The place was filled with the sound of vendors hawking their wares, mixed with the shuffle and hustle of a stew mix of L.A. life—business guys grabbing a quick bite, mamas buying food for their families, street people looking for handouts or trays with food left on them, kids hoping for ice cream. The aroma of taco meat and fresh coffee fought off the smells drifting in from Broadway on one side and Hill on the other.

There was a seat open at the China Cafe counter between an ample gent invading my elbow space and a guy wearing a backwards Dodgers cap who was working on some egg foo young.

I ordered chop suey and a lemonade. Halfway through I called Ira and told him about my meetings at Sonhouse, and that they'd take Coby on a provisional basis.

"Arraignment tomorrow morning," Ira said. "You want to sleep over?"

"Ooh. Can we make a tent and read comic books?"

"Just don't annoy me."

"Where's the fun in that?"

"Oy vey," Ira said.

I keep a change of clothes at Ira's for just such a time as this. Beats driving back to the Cove then all the way back to Ira's in the morning if we have something downtown.

We had time for a game of chess. I was black and boggled his mind with my first move.

"Center Counter Game, eh?" Ira said.

"No prisoners," I said. The Center Counter is rarely used by grandmasters, as it costs Black an inferior pawn structure in return for greater freedom for the pieces. Black hopes for a counter attack to neutralize White's powerful center pawn. The lines have all led to a slight advantage for White. But since it is so rare, it's not prepped for and a good player can catch White off guard.

"Going to bring out your queen early?" Ira said.

"Take me and find out," I said.

He took my pawn. I took his pawn with my queen. He brought out his knight to threaten my queen. I moved my queen to a5.

"Cheeky," Ira said.

"Are those beads of sweat I see on your forehead?" I said.

"Those are ice crystals," Ira said.

"We shall see."

Twenty-one moves later he checkmated me.

By then it was Ira's tea time. Ira loves his tea. I force myself to drink some because of my charitable spirit, and because it pleases Ira, even though he knows I prefer coffee.

We sat near the bay window.

"Any strategy we need to discuss?" I said.

"For what?" Ira said.

"The arraignment, of course."

"Ah. I thought you meant life."

"You did not."

"Regardless, what is your strategy on that score?"

"Life," I said, "is the art of drawing sufficient conclusions from insufficient premises."

"Who said that?"

"It was either Samuel Butler or Francis the Talking Mule."

"With whom you identify," Ira said.

"Butler?" I said.

"The mule."

I didn't do a lot of talking after that.

. . .

I slept in the guest room, which is really my room, the place I lived when I first got to L.A., getting as far away from the past as I could. The past caught up with me, of course. It has a way of doing that. But now I was in a state of rough equilibrium. Investigating for Ira on a case as simple as Coby Keaton's was going to be, in the scheme of things, rather placid. I mean, what could go wrong?

Do not ever ask that question.

A rraignment court downtown is a hive of activity, buzzing with impatient lawyers, anxious mothers or girlfriends, weary bailiffs, and grumpy clerks. Then there's the arrestees, some in street clothes, others in jailhouse blues with the occasional orange for the higher security defendants. A cluster of them sat in the jury box awaiting their names to be called.

Coby was one of them. He looked tired and nervous.

I sat in the gallery taking it all in. It was like the circus, back before the busybodies ruined circuses. Now the animals were in the jury box, chained, and Coby looked like a monkey among lions. I almost had a hankering for a bag of popcorn.

Ira sat on a chair inside the bar, chatting with another lawyer. An arraignment deputy from the DA's office stood at the prosecutor's table going through a stack of files.

The nameplate on the judge's bench said *Hon. Myron Maltz.*

A little after eight-thirty the bailiff said, "All rise. The Superior Court of California, County of Los Angeles, is now in session. The Honorable Judge Myron Maltz presiding." Maltz entered and took his chair. His thick hair and bushy eyebrows were the same color as his robe, giving the impression of an Italian monk in 1542 about to call the Inquisition to order.

He asked for the People—that's what they call the prosecution in California—to state his appearance for the record.

The arraignment deputy was young, no doubt given this assignment because he was relatively new to the office. He said, "Stuart Propp for the People, Your Honor."

And we were off. Cases were called, pleas entered, defendants marched back to the lockup.

Coby's name was sixth or seventh.

Ira stood, using his braces to get to the defense table. A deputy sheriff had Coby stand in the jury box.

"Good morning, Your Honor. Ira Rosen appearing on behalf of Coby Keaton. We waive a reading of the complaint and statement of rights, and enter a plea of not guilty. In lieu of bail, we request diversion."

Judge Maltz said, "Mr. Propp?"

"The defendant has no ties to the community, Your Honor. He's a flight risk."

"Mr. Rosen?" said the judge.

"That's but one factor under *Humphrey*, Your Honor," Ira said. "Consider that Mr. Keaton has a minor criminal record, a DUI in Las Vegas, for which he made his appearance and was diverted to an alcohol treatment program, which program he completed. Further, we have arranged for Mr. Keaton to find housing with the Sonhouse Rescue Mission."

"Tatum Walker does good work," Judge Maltz said. "Do you have an objection, Mr. Propp?"

"Yes, we do," said Propp, but without enthusiasm.

"All right," said Maltz. "Objection overruled. Mr. Keaton will be placed in Sonhouse. Mr. Rosen, you'll forward to the court a certified copy of the reception paper?"

"I will, Your Honor."

"Good." The judge looked at his monitor. He called out a date for the preliminary hearing. Propp and Ira agreed to it.

.   .   .

W e talked to Coby in the lockup.
Ira said, "Be on your best behavior at Sonhouse."
"I will," Coby said.

"I'm going to talk to the prosecutor," Ira said. "I don't see why this can't be settled as a misdemeanor knife carry."

"Settled?" Coby said.

"No trial, no jail," Ira said. "You'll get some hours of community service, but can do it out of Sonhouse."

"I'll take it!" Coby said. "Thanks, Mr. Rosen. You know, I was going to tell you a time travel joke."

"Oh?" Ira said.

"Yeah," Coby said. "But you didn't like it."

"Keep 'em laughing, Coby," Ira said.

I ra went home. I waited for Coby to get processed, then walked him to Sonhouse. As we headed down Hill Street, Coby said, "My dad played trombone in Vegas orchestras. Barry Manilow, Rod Stewart, The Righteous Brothers. He wanted me to play piano but I didn't take to it. He put all his attention on my sister. I'm pretty worthless in his eyes. When I was, I don't know, eight or nine I snuck in and saw Jerry Seinfeld at Caesars Palace. I thought that was so amazing, that he was making hundreds of people laugh, one joke right after the other. People loved him. I wanted people to love me too, so that's when I decided to try to make it as a comedian, but I had to leave Vegas 'cause my dad didn't want me around. I needed to try to come out here and make it on my own. I don't know. Do you think I have a shot?"

"Not if you keep getting baked," I said.

"Huh?"

"No more weed."

"Aw, come on, that's not what I need to hear."

I stopped and grabbed his shoulders. "You want to be a comedian? You want to stick around a while? Then take care of your brain. That's where the money is. You put today's ganja in it and you'll gum it up, beyond repair. You think Groucho Marx smoked weed?"

"I don't know that much about him."

"And you call yourself a comedian," I said. "How can you not know about Groucho Marx?"

"You're making me feel bad," Coby said.

"Ask me if I care," I said.

"Huh?"

"It doesn't matter how you feel," I said. "It matters what you do, and what you stop yourself from doing. Get that into your head, and not that other stuff. Now start walking."

We crossed Second Street.

"How you fixed for clothes?" I said.

"I got some," Coby said.

"Condition?"

"Enough to wear."

"Let's pad that. Where's the nearest thrift store?"

"There's one on 12th," Coby said.

"We're taking a walk to 12th," I said.

It was a journey through people and things and trash and a needle every so often. Every now and then Coby would make a remark about this or that store or corner.

Once he got a glare from a blinged-out dude playing lookout for a drug deal. You get to know the profile. It's like a meerkat looking up for predatory birds. Coby lowered his head and speeded up his walk.

"Friend of yours?" I said.

"Bad guy," Coby said.

"You in to him for anything?"

"No way, I don't do that street stuff."

"Keep it that way," I said.

The thrift store was a pretty good size. I told Coby to pick out a couple pairs of jeans, a couple shirts, some packaged underwear and socks. Also a pair of used Converse All Star sneakers. I paid for it at the counter and they put it all in a big bag.

"Why're you doing this?" Coby asked.

"You're a client," I said.

"But I should be paying you, not the other way around."

"We're on the county dime," I said. "So don't worry about it."

As we walked out of the store, Coby's head hung low.

"What's the matter?" I said.

"Nobody's ever been this nice to me," he said.

"It's called the complete Ira Rosen-Mike Romeo treatment, kid," I said. "All you have to do is keep your nose clean."

"Hey, what do you call a nose with no body?" Coby said.

"I have a feeling you're going to tell me."

"Nobody nose," Coby said.

I pushed him toward the door.

At Sonhouse, Tommy Thompson and Nathan White came out to the front desk to check Coby in. Coby was nervous. Nathan White, who was close to Coby's age, put a hand on his shoulder. "No worries, Coby," he said. "We're here to make your stay as comfortable as possible. Anything you need, you're going to let me know, okay?"

"Okay," Coby said. "Thanks."

Tommy Thompson said, "Welcome to Sonhouse, Mr. Keaton."

"Wow," Coby said. "I haven't been called mister in a long time. I've been called other things." Coby forced a smile.

"What would you like us to call you?" Thompson asked.

"Anything you want," Coby said. "Just don't call me late for dinner."

"Ba-dump-bump," I said. "Coby will do, right, Coby?"

"Yes," Coby said.

"Then I'll be off," I said. I gave Coby a pat on the back. "Good luck. We'll be in touch."

As Thompson and White escorted Coby into the facility, he looked back at me over his shoulder. I felt like a daddy dropping off his kid for the first day of school.

"What are you doing?" Sophie said.

It was late afternoon and we were eating at Urban Plates. Fat Burger had been an option, but we were both in training. Sophie was going to be running a 5k in a couple of weeks. I was getting ready for a three-round sparring match at Jimmy Sarducci's gym. So it was Asian chicken noodle salad for her and chimichurri steak for me.

"I'm making eyes at you," I said. I bobbed my eyebrows a couple of times.

"You're what?" Sophie said.

"I was advised to find a girl and make eyes at her," I said.

"Who, may I ask, advised you on this course of action?"

"Mrs. Edna Morgenstern, Ira's next-door neighbor. She was married to Sammy for fifty-two years. She told me I have to find a girl and make eyes at her. So here we are."

Sophie smiled. "And where, exactly, is that?"

It was the right question, the one neither of us could answer with any certainty. Too many *ifs* and *buts*. Not enough *ands* and *definitelys*. One of the biggest obstacles was how I lived my life. I worked for Ira, who takes on cases to set things right in this world. This was my drive, too. Insatiable it seemed. Why? Maybe to salve the wounds—and guilt—of my past. Whatever the source, it brought trouble, sometimes lots of it. Could I in good conscience pull a woman as vital as Sophie into that net? I had my doubts. So I asked—

"What if I settled down?"

"You?" Sophie said.

"Why not?"

"What would that even look like?" she said. "I'm trying to picture it."

"Picture me sitting on a porch in a rocking chair, whittling," I said.

"Right."

"You sound skeptical."

"Romeo, you could no more sit and whittle than a wolf could play footsie with a lamb."

I almost choked on a bite of steak. She had me nailed.

"Who in their right mind would hitch their wagon to me?" I said.

"Do you think my mind is right?" Sophie said.

"Righter than most," I said. "Because you're doing the most important work there is, directing young minds to the eternal verities."

"I find it equally challenging to know what's going on in the mind of Mike Romeo," Sophie said.

"It's a mine field," I said.

"Meaning, step carefully?"

"Or don't step at all." Sophie looked down at her plate and said nothing.

"I didn't mean that," I said.

"No?" Sophie said.

"No."

"Then let me in," she said.

"Ira and I have a new client," I said. "A kid named Coby Keaton. Wants to be a standup comedian. He's been living on the street, and a few days ago he knifed a guy to death."

Sophie put her hand on her chest.

I said, "The guy he killed was somebody he'd been sharing a tent with. According to Coby, the guy was out of his mind, naked on the street, and was choking him."

"Doesn't that make it self defense?" Sophie said.

"It does, but right now we need to gather more facts. There's more."

I told her about "Lucifer is coming" and Tatum Walker's view of what was happening in the world.

"Wow," Sophie said. "That kind of makes sense, considering all that's going on." She paused, then added, "Do you believe there's a real devil?"

"There are more things in Heaven and Earth, Horatio, than are dreamt of in your philosophy."

"Hamlet," Sophie said. "Doesn't he say that right after seeing his father's ghost?"

"Exactly."

"Meaning there's more going on than we can access through philosophy," Sophie said. "Maybe ghosts and devils really exist."

"We can't rule it out," I said.

"This is cheery," Sophie said.

"And there's your peek into the mind of Romeo," I said. "Care to stick around?"

She smiled, lowered her head, and looked at me with a narrowed gaze.

"What's this?" I said.

"I'm making eyes at *you*," she said.

"You do that very nicely," I said.

F riday morning was cold and dreary at Paradise Cove. I did my polar-bear swim, appreciating all the more the fur and blubber of those Arctic inhabitants. I should have felt sharp and ready to do some digging for facts. But the gray dampness of the fog filled me with a sense of dread. I hate that feeling, like something bad is about to happen. Because it usually does.

Two hours later I was downtown. I parked in a lot on Los Angeles Street, near the corner of Third. I walked to the intersection where Coby had seen the naked Zon screaming at cars. There were several small shops on the road. A cut-rate electronics store, a wholesale vacuum place, a store selling socks, T-shirts and underwear *For Less*.

I tried the electronics place first. It was a thin corridor with shelves on either side, stuffed with older model cell phones, tablets, headphones, speakers, monitors, open boxes with cables and adapters, and other unbranded gadgets and gizmos. It was a cafeteria for shoplifters, but since L.A. wasn't prosecuting them anymore, thieves preferred to go to high end places for the latest in electric booty. Somewhere a radio blared Salsa music.

In the middle of the place was a glass case with more gadgets. A man behind the case, wearing a gray guayabera and black pants, looked at me.

I went up and nodded at him. He nodded back.

"Can I ask you a question?" I said.

"*Qué?*" he said.

"Question. *Pregunta.*"

He nodded.

My Spanish was about used up. "The killing outside." I pointed to the street. "A week ago?"

He shrugged like he didn't understand.

"Out there," I said. I made a motion like I was stabbing myself. I felt like an idiot tourist in Bolivia.

He shook his head.

I took out my phone and brought up the pic of Coby I'd taken at the jail.

He looked at it. Shook his head.

Even if he'd seen something I wasn't going to get any

information out of him.

Next, I went to the discount socks and underwear place. All sorts of garments in plastic bags. No music. The Salsa beat from next door was loud enough.

The proprietor was an Asian man who smiled at me. It was a good start.

It didn't last.

"Hello," I said, to test the waters.

"Ha," he said. He could have meant *Hi.*

"Can I ask you a question?"

"Question, yeah, okay."

"There was a killing just outside your store about a week ago."

He frowned, then nodded. "Yeah, yeah, very bad. Yeah."

"Did you see what happened?"

"Oh, yeah, yeah."

"Can you tell me what you saw?"

He started to think about it, then looked over my shoulder, his face registering immediate concern.

I turned and saw a guy in shades and a Las Vegas Raiders jersey sauntering in. He was about my size. He came right up, smiling, nodding at the proprietor. Then turned his gaze to me.

"Hey, bruh," he said. "Mind steppin' out for a minute? Got some business to talk over."

From the look on the store man's face, I knew it wasn't legit business. I eliminated a drug transaction. I sensed something like protection money.

"I'm buying some underwear," I said.

"Come back later."

I glanced at his waist and saw a bulge under the jersey.

"You go," Store Guy said to me, his voice shaky.

I wasn't about to go.

"Why don't I buy my underwear," I said to the Raider, "and we can go outside and discuss this?"

That brought out the full fury of the street. He got in my face and started with mother-effing this and mother-effing that. I cut him off at the third mother by giving him a full elbow to the nose.

Crushing a nose does not, as some think, send cartilage to the brain and induce death. It does, as my old MMA coach used to say, make a guy smell his own thoughts. Down he went.

"No, no!" Store Guy said.

I dropped and lifted the jersey and took out the gun in the thug's waistband. A nine. I pulled the slide and saw a round was chambered.

"No!" Store Guy was waving his arms, jumping up and down. "No!"

I went behind the counter and grabbed him by the shirt.

"Shut up!" I pulled him out and shoved him toward the door. "Go outside and run, then call the police."

"No!"

"Go!"

"No!"

Not my idea of a constructive conversation.

I put the gun in my waistband and flopped my Hawaiian shirt over it. I walked out and fell in with the street crowd. I hoofed to the parking garage, got in Spinoza, and drove away from Crazy Town.

I was in a dark fog even though the sun was shining. My tires burned the street when I braked in front of Ira's. My sneakers burned the floor as I barged through his front door.

"Whoa!" Ira said, looking up from his desk.

Without a word I went to the kitchen, turned on the faucet, and slapped my face with water.

"I sense something amiss," Ira said.

I couldn't dance with him. "I beat up a guy," I said.

"You did what?" Ira said.

"Beat up," I said. "A guy."

"Michael..."

That tone. "Don't Ira, just don't."

I grabbed a dish towel and patted my face, went back to the front room.

Where Ira gave me that penetrating gaze of his. It's a laser that cuts through any barrier I try to set up. Resistance is futile.

I said, "This guy was collecting protection money from a man running an underwear store."

"Excuse me?"

"I was talking to the store guy about Coby and Zon. He saw something. But before I could get it, this guy packing a gun comes in."

"You saw the gun?"

"The bulge. He got in my grill so I put him down."

"Down how?"

I mimed an elbow strike.

"Go on," Ira said.

"I told the store guy to call the police, but he freaked out."

"Anybody witness this, besides the proprietor?"

"No."

"What happened to the gun?"

I pulled it out of my waistband and gave it to him.

Ira looked it over. "A 9mm semi-automatic. I know this company. They supply Argentina's armed forces. Reasonably priced, too, which is why it's popular in Central and South America. And why it's showing up on the streets of Chicago. And now, apparently, in L.A."

"I'm going to keep it," I said.

"That's not a good idea," Ira said.

"We've had this talk before," I said. "I'm willing to risk it.

It won't be one of yours that I'm carrying around."

"Small consolation," Ira said.

"Would you rather have a live felon or a dead investigator?"

"This store," Ira said. "Likely there's security footage."

"I don't think so," I said. "If they're paying protection, the collectors wouldn't allow it."

"Good point," Ira said. "But you'll be described."

"So what? I'm on the right side of this one."

"So report this," Ira said.

"No."

"Michael, you have to—"

"I don't have to do anything. Let them sort it out. Let them find me if they can."

"That's no way to—"

"It's the only way," I said.

Ira got that rabbi look on his face. "I will remind you of the Book of Leviticus, chapter five, verse one. If a person does not come forward to testify regarding something of legal importance that he has seen, he will be held responsible. In such a matter you are not permitted to remain silent."

"Oh yeah?" I said. "The Book of Romeo says you don't owe the truth to people who lie. And something like this is always lied about."

"Michael—"

"Goodbye, Ira."

I drove back to the Cove in the same dark fog as before. The thought of having to tell Sophie about all this scorched my insides.

As usual, a hard swim in the chop cooled things a little.

I showered and plopped on the futon with my laptop and a Corona, and checked the news.

Never a dull moment in the Golden State, which should be renamed the Dull Pewter State. The powers that be have driven all the gold out of it.

Up in San Francisco a clothing store filed a lawsuit against the prior owners of the retail space in Union Square for failing to uphold terms outlined in their lease agreement. What was the problem? A little thing called "rampant criminal activity." They had to close the store because employees were faced with repeated thefts and violence. And what was described as "aggressive guests." I guess when somebody comes in wielding a machete that could fit as aggressive.

But the lease they signed required the landlord to allow the store to "peaceably and quietly hold and enjoy the premises without hindrance or interruption." I guess smash-and-grab thefts don't fall into the peace and quiet category. But who knows in the current climate? Maybe it's all relative.

In any event, the landlord, rather than take steps to mitigate the damage, just decided to walk away from the retail space and default on their $500 million loan.

That's called doing business in the Dull Pewter State.

Closer to home, meaning Los Angeles, politicians were jockeying for position for the next mayoral race. The story profiled a couple of names, including a guy named Duncan Caldwell. Caldwell caught my attention. He was the owner of a couple of car dealerships and was running on a "make the streets safe" platform. He said he was partnering with Tatum Walker.

I made a mental note of that.

Fed up with the news, I chose a book to get into. That's always my preferred way of crowding out thoughts I did not wish to entertain. This time I chose *Fahrenheit 451*. Now was the time to revisit Bradbury's classic. It's all about book burning as a metaphor for keeping the people from thinking for themselves, for discovering truths that the government does not like, to mold them and control them, to besot them with visual "reality."

Like it was written yesterday.

I'd forgotten the hero's name was Montag. That's Sophie's last name. That got random thoughts swirling again.

I got to the part where Montag is walking with Clarisse— telling her how wonderful it was to burn Millay, Whitman, and Faulkner to ashes—when I got a call from Ira.

"How you doing, boy?" he said.

"Other than wanting to take a flamethrower to Los Angeles, I'm pretty good," I said.

"Seriously, Michael."

"Don't worry," I said. "I've got a beer and a book. I'll be fine."

"I need you to be fine, okay?"

"Yes, rabbi."

"Because something's come up. Coby's missing."

"What?"

"I got a call from Sonhouse asking if I knew where he was. He was checked in and went to his first meeting. He went to bed. He was supposed to meet with his counselor in the morning, a fellow named Thompson."

"Yeah, I met him."

"He never showed up," Ira said. "They looked for him. No sign of him anywhere."

"Terrific."

"Why don't you go there tomorrow and see if you can figure out what happened."

"Me and downtown don't mix," I said.

"Don't take the gun," Ira said.

"Do I seem that reckless to you?"

"You want a straight answer?"

"Not really."

"The answer is yes," Ira said.

"Why do you do it, Ira?"

"Do what?"

"Look out for me," I said.

"It's a habit," he said. "Someday I'll break through that impenetrable wall of yours."

"Like the walls of Jericho?"

"Good for you, quoting the Bible," Ira said.

"Just don't blow a trumpet in my ear."

"Not promising anything," Ira said.

Next morning I swam, did a hundred pushups on the sand, then made myself an omelet, chased with two cups of coffee. It didn't settle well.

Around ten I drove to Sonhouse. Traffic was a bear, which isn't news. There was an accident on the 101 just past the 405. A white Prius was on its side, smashed like an accordion. A big black SUV was behind it, messed up. An ambulance was on the scene. I tried to pretend this wasn't symbolic.

It was a full two hours before I made it to Sonhouse.

The guy at the front desk, a fortyish man in a T-shirt and overalls, said, "You're back. Guess you heard about Coby."

"Any sign of him?" I said.

He shook his head.

"Is Reverend Walker around?"

"Don't think so. You can check the office."

"Thanks." I started to go.

"Hey," the guy said.

I turned back.

"Hope you find him," he said. "He's a good kid. And funny."

I walked down the hall and knocked on Tatum Walker's office door. No answer. I walked on to the double doors at the end of the hall, and went through into the dining area.

A few men of various ages and looks, yet with a similarity that street denizen seem to share, sat at some tables. It wasn't meal time. There was a card game going on with three guys, two chess games, and one guy slapping the table like he was playing drums.

I went to one of the chess boards. One of the players was north of sixty years old and had three days' growth of stubble on his face. He rubbed his chin as he studied the board.

The other guy was in his twenties and had the intense look of a defuser studying a bomb.

The guy with the stubble looked at me and smiled. Which told me it was the younger guy's move. I looked at the board. I was a pretty fair chess player once. I saw that the young man was caught in a knight fork. That's where a knight is simultaneously attacking two pieces at once. The kid had to decide which piece he was going to lose.

"Gotcha, Milo," Stubble said.

Milo said nothing.

Stubble looked at me and said, "You new here?"

"I work for a lawyer," I said. "We represent Coby Keaton, but he's apparently gone missing."

"Who?"

"Coby Keaton. Long hair, skinny. Makes jokes."

"Oh yeah, him," Stubble said. "He wasn't here too long."

Milo appeared frozen.

"Try bishop to E6," I said.

The youngster shot me a look.

"You'll at least get a pawn back," I said.

"Hey!" Stubble said.

"Thanks, man," Milo said.

Another voice said, "Excuse me." It was Nathan White, the young man who worked with Thompson. He had concern all over his face. "Can I help you?"

"I'm trying to find out what happened to Coby Keaton," I said. "Do you know?"

Nathan shook his head. "It happens, more than we'd like. Guys don't like the discipline, guys want drugs, they just up and leave."

"Was there any indication Coby was unhappy here?"

"Not that I saw," Nathan said.

"Is Mr. Thompson around?"

"Um…"

I waited.

"Can I see him?" I said.

"I'm not sure."

"Can you check?"

"Um…"

"Or shall I just go hunting for him?"

"Mr. Romeo—"

"Kid, we're on the same team here. Is he in or not?"

"I'll tell him you're here," he said. "Can I get you something? Coffee?"

"Water would be nice," I said.

He nodded and scurried off.

Meanwhile, the young guy had made the move I suggested. Stubble was now looking at the board, grumbling.

Nathan White returned, handed me a cup of water, and motioned for me to follow.

Thompson was in his office at his desk. Nathan White left and closed the door.

"I wonder," Tommy Thompson said, "if it's good for you to be here."

"Why do you wonder that?" I said.

"It's causing some nerves."

"What does that mean?"

"Well, you know, we all know what went down with Coby and Zon. But do we really need it rubbed in our faces?"

"You think that's what I'm doing?"

"I don't mean it that way, Mr. Romeo,"

"Tell me exactly what you mean, Mr. Thompson."

"There's a lot of uncertainty down here," Thompson said. "People don't know from one day to the next how they'll end up. Our first job is to give them hope. Without that, nothing else matters."

"There's still a real world out there," I said. "I'm sure everyone here understands that. And right now I have a real-world job to do."

"Fine," he said. "But I don't have that much to tell you. Coby and I met when he first got here. I gave him a rundown on how we do things here and what we expect from him. Things like keeping his room clean, no drugs or alcohol, attending chapel. He seemed happy to be here. He was at chapel in the afternoon. He even volunteered to do KP after dinner. He'd already made some friends. I guess he's pretty good at making people laugh. But in the morning he didn't come to breakfast. I went to check his room."

"What time was that?" I said.

"Around eleven. I knocked on the door, there was no answer. The door was unlocked. I looked inside. The bed was messy, but Coby wasn't there."

"You have any idea where he might have gone?" I said.

Thompson waved his arm. "Out there. The streets. He could be anywhere."

"Who were those friends you mentioned?" I said.

"Why do you ask?"

"Why do you think? Maybe they know something."

He drummed his fingers on the desk. "Can you allow me some time to gather that information?"

"How much time?"

"I can't really say," he said. "But I'll do it. I promise."

"If he comes back," I said, "will you call me immediately?"

"Of course," Thompson said. "And maybe calling is how we should communicate from now on."

"Meaning you don't want me around."

"I just think it would be better."

"I'll take that up with Rev. Walker," I said.

"He's not here right now."

"Then I'll just have to come back later."

Thompson stood. "I'm sorry to be so abrupt."

"I've been known to be abrupt myself," I said.

Abruptly, I left.

M y GPS told me the freeway was still jammed. So I took Wilshire across town. I like doing that anyway, getting to know my adopted city. Wilshire used to be a glamorous street, with Art Deco buildings like the Bullock's Wilshire, and magnificent churches like Immanuel Presbyterian. Now they all seemed like old men gathered in a park, talking about better times, livelier times, and jawing about their recent surgeries.

Then you roll by the La Brea Tar Pits, where wooly mammoths got stuck.

There used to be classy restaurants here, like the Brown Derby. Now you've got Mickey D's and Jersey Mike's.

It was just past San Vicente that I noticed a tail. I might have missed it with all the sightseeing I was doing. But I happened to notice in my rearview a sedan with tinted windows, two cars behind me. Illegal tint. So I kept checking it as I drove on. The sedan made an effort to keep that two-car space, even as the cars in between us changed. A classic, professional technique. As Joey Feint, the New Haven PI I worked for long ago, taught me, you don't want to be right behind your mark. Too easy to spot that way.

A simple way to make sure you're being followed is to make a couple of turns.

I did.

And was followed.

I pulled into a strip mall and found a spot to park. Didn't see the car. But it could have been waiting for me to pull out again. There was a Korean market in front of me. I strolled in and walked to the back. An *Employees Only* sign was posted by a door with plastic flaps. Well, I was employed by Ira Rosen, so I went through. A cluttered office was to the left, and a bathroom to the right. At the back was a door. I went through and into an alley. I walked down to the cross street. On the way I picked up an empty beer can by a dumpster. Bud Light. I felt sorry for whoever drank it.

I came around the block and saw the car parked there. I took a picture of the license plate, then threw the beer can at the back window.

A woman got out. She was in her thirties, dressed in business casual. Her hair was nicely done. She was nicely put together, too.

"Car trouble?" I said.

She cut me with her eyes, but kept her cool. "Back off," she said.

"I could say the same to you."

"I don't know what you're talking about."

"Don't do that," I said. "I love my intelligence and don't like it to be insulted. Why are you following me?"

She looked at the sky. A poker player she wasn't.

"Don't take it too hard," I said. "Your technique is actually pretty good. You've had training. You an undercover cop, or an ex doing private work?"

She said nothing.

"You're obviously working for somebody," I said. "Unless it's your practice to target ruggedly handsome guys driving cool cars."

Her face almost broke into a smile. It wanted to. But professional caution put the brakes on that.

"Maybe we can put this whole thing to bed," I said, immediately wishing I'd chose different language. "I mean—"

"I know what you mean," she said. "Cards on the table?"

"Something like that."

She nodded. "Not here on the street."

"There's a coffee place in the strip mall. My treat."

"Okay," she said. "I'll pull in."

As she got in her car I walked up the street to the mall. The coffee place was really a donut shop that had a sign in the window that read *Fresh, hot coffee.* At the driveway in I paused and waited for her to enter.

But she hit the gas and drove right on by.

It was my turn to look at the sky.

I went in the donut place and ordered a coffee and an apple fritter. To heck with training. If life hands you lemons, eat fried dough. I sat at a table and sent Ira the picture of the car. Five minutes later I called him.

"Now why would a rented luxury car be following little old me?" I said.

"To keep from being traced to someone who does not wish to be traced," Ira said.

"Someone with deep pockets," I said. "A luxury car for tailing a guy?"

"Perhaps this young woman picks people up at airports, too."

"She didn't strike me as the chauffeur type. Her technique was professional."

"Undercover cop?"

"In a luxury rental? With illegally tinted windows?"

"Illegal you say?"

"The front windshield was completely covered. What's the law on that?"

"Ah. Four inches at the top only. But it's not a hanging offense."

"What is these days?" I said.

"The point is, the police aren't going to spend any time trying to get to the bottom of something so trivial."

"Especially since they don't seem to bother getting to the bottom of shoplifting or smash-and-grabs."

"I'll see if I can find anything in the Eminence computer system," Ira said.

"Isn't hacking against the law?" I said.

"In California the crime of unauthorized computer access, or hacking, contains the element of harm. That means tampering, interference, or damage. Like what those hackers did to the MGM Resorts in Las Vegas."

"Do tell."

"They hacked in and held up all operations at the hotels. MGM owns the Bellagio, the NoMad, Mandalay Bay, and, of course, the MGM Grand. For ten days, these places couldn't operate per normal, like accessing reservations or even issuing key cards for the rooms. Not only that, tens of millions of records were breached, including driver's licenses and Social Security numbers. That's what you call a crime."

"How'd they get out of it?"

"Paid the ransom."

"How much?"

"A guess is fifty million."

"That's not hay," I said.

"On the other hand," said Ira, "MGM resorts makes about fourteen billion, with a B, per year."

"Are you underpaying me, Ira?"

"Your ability to string together thoughts is a wonder to behold."

"Now, now. Sarcasm is unbecoming a rabbi."

"Not so, my boy. You've heard of Elijah taunting the prophets of Baal on Mount Carmel?"

"I seem to recall something," I said.

"It was a contest of the gods," Ira said. "Who would rain fire, Baal or Yahweh? As the Baal prophets cried out for hours around their altar, Elijah began chiding them. Cry louder, he said. Perhaps your god is asleep. Maybe he is—to clean up the language a bit—taking a dump."

"He did not say that."

"He said exactly that in ancient Hebrew."

"A smack-talking prophet," I said. "I like it."

"When the fire did not appear, Elijah built an altar using twelve stones. He put on wood and the carcass of a bull. Then he ordered the whole thing soaked with water. He stood back and called to God. And fire rained down and burned up the sacrifice, the wood, the stones and all the water."

"Nice," I said. "I want to do that sometime."

"Talk trash?" Ira said.

"Rain fire," I said.

"I advise you to hit the heavy bag instead."

"I'll think about it," I said.

I did think about it, driving to the Valley. On the way, I called Coltrane Smith, an LAPD detective I knew. I explained to him about the missing Coby, and asked what could be done about it.

He said, "If there's evidence the person left voluntarily, we're not going to allocate resources. Adults have the legal right to go missing if they choose to do so."

"No evidence one way or the other," I said.

"Well, if the evidence is limited or unclear, that's not enough to go forward. You know as well as I do that we have to prioritize cases based on perceived level of risk and urgency."

"Sure."

"Sorry to be the bearer of bad news."

"No problem," I said. "It was worth a shot."

"Give it a few days, see if you can shake anything else out."

"Shaking is what I do," I said.

He laughed. "I know that to be true." He paused. "You know who you might try to talk to? Somebody with the Duncan Caldwell campaign."

"The mayor candidate," I said. "I read about him. He's got some sort of connection with Tatum Walker."

"He's all over the homeless issue," Coltrane said. "And he has contacts on the street. Might be that his people would want to help on this."

"For political reasons."

"Mike, it is possible that a politician really believes what he's saying."

"It's possible to believe in singing unicorns, too."

"You really are a cynic."

"But with charm," I said.

"Don't oversell yourself," Coltrane Smith said.

Jimmy Sarducci is a short, pugnacious owner of a gym in the Valley. He trains fighters in what he continues to call "the sweet science." That's what they used to call boxing, back in the day when fighters like Sugar Ray Robinson treated the sport like an art, a skill, and not just a slugfest. He's always at me to make a comeback in the ring, even though my background is not the boxing ring but the octagon.

He's done me a lot of favors, so I said I'd come in sometime and work out with one of his fighters. I need to keep in shape, and the occasional sparring match is the best workout for fighting trim.

In the locker room, Jimmy taped my hands. "He's a good young fighter," he said. "I need him to learn to be more than a puncher."

"Good," I said. "Tell him not to throw any punches."

Jimmy snorted. He slipped 18-ounce gloves on me and laced them up.

"Dance with him," Jimmy said.

"What if he doesn't hear the music?" I said.

Jimmy put a head guard on me. "Then you're on your own," he said.

"What are you still doing in the fight game, Jimmy? Nobody respects it anymore."

"I respect it," he said, his eyes flashing. "My dad respected it, he raised me to respect it. There's a lot of worms in it crawling around, but if you can get one good fighter . . . and save these kids. The worms don't care if kids get their brains mashed because they can't box. Somebody's got to help 'em and as long as I got breath, I'm gonna."

"That's a good answer, Jimmy."

"It's all I got. That, alimony, and a few good prospects."

"Let's have a look," I said.

The other fighter was already in the ring. Jimmy and I went through the ropes, and Jimmy waved him over.

"This is Jeremiah Diggs," Jimmy said.

"Mike Romeo," I said and put out a glove. Diggs ignored

it. He was in his early twenties, and ripped. His expression was sour, like a tiger with acid reflux.

"Let's do this," Diggs said and went to the opposite corner.

"Friendly chap," I said to Jimmy.

Jimmy grunted and stepped out of the ring. He held up the stopwatch hanging from a string around his neck, and said, "Go!"

Diggs charged like we were in Madison Square Garden on a pay-per-view deal. He didn't bother with a jab. He threw a right at my head. I fended it off with my left, but his punch was strong enough to knock my own glove into my chin.

There's an unwritten rule about sparring. You don't go a hundred percent. You're not trying for a win. You're building skills.

This was a rule Jeremiah Diggs apparently did not know. Or chose to ignore.

He landed a left to my gut. The guy had power.

I jabbed him and backed up.

"Easy, tiger," I said.

"Ain't no easy about it," Diggs said.

"Stick and move!" Jimmy said.

Diggs did not stick, but he did move. Fast. He came at me with a flurry of punches. I defended. And started to get mad.

"Hose him down, Jimmy," I said.

"Easy, Jeremiah!" Jimmy said.

"Ain't no easy," Diggs said. He started to circle. His eyes had knockout in them.

I wanted to take him down with a grapple, hold his windpipe, and make him tap out. But this was boxing. I remembered a tip that if you've got a bull-rush opponent, don't waste energy dancing around the ring. Take a step and pivot out of the way. You're like a matador. You swivel and let the bull pass by, and hit him as he does.

Diggs came at me. I pivoted and tagged his face with my left. A good one. He stumbled into the ropes.

And looked surprised.

I floated like a butterfly to the center of the ring. But Jimmy didn't want me to sting like a bee.

So I said, "Show me some skills."

I expected him to say "Ain't no skills."

But he said nothing. He charged me once more, wildly punching.

"Easy!" Jimmy said. "Stick and move!"

Hands up, elbows down, I went to pure defense.

Then he got me. A right that rearranged the furniture in my head. I went down on one knee.

Which should have been the end of it.

But Diggs gave me another blow to the back of my head. Next thing I knew I was sniffing canvas.

"Stop!" Jimmy said. "Time!"

Fire filled me. It shot me to my knees, then my feet.

Diggs attacked.

Jimmy shouted, "No!"

I put the full fury of my left into Diggs's ribs.

He went *Oof.*

And then Romeo's Hammer, my right, smashed his face.

He fell like a sack of wet towels.

"No, no!" Jimmy clambered through the ropes.

Diggs, flat, looked up, eyes glazed.

Jimmy knelt next to his fighter.

"Non est gloria in stultitia," I said.

Diggs blinked.

I gave him the rough translation. "Ain't no glory in being a fool," I said.

. . .

I showered and dressed. Jimmy was in his office, talking to Diggs, when I popped in to say goodbye. Diggs was still in his boxing shorts and white T-shirt.

"Hey, man," Diggs said. "Look, I kinda lost it in there."

"No big thing," I said. "Forget about it."

I put out my hand and we shook.

"You got a punch," Diggs said.

"So do you," I said. "So listen to Jimmy and learn the art. Put that together with your power, and you've got massive upside."

"What I been tellin' him," Jimmy said.

"You told him about Gentleman Jim and Jake LaMotta?" I said.

"You tell him," Jimmy said.

"Gentleman Jim Corbett was heavyweight champ, beat John L. Sullivan. Because he could dance and box. Really, the first to do it. He left the fight game with his good looks and mind intact. LaMotta's head was a punching bag, he wouldn't go down, and he got facial rearrangement in most of his fights. You've got a good face, Diggs. Keep it that way."

Diggs smiled.

My phone buzzed. It was Ira. "Gotta take this," I said, waved, and went outside Jimmy's office.

"You sitting down?" Ira said.

"Walking," I said.

"Tommy Thompson, at Sonhouse…"

"Yeah."

"He's dead."

I stopped walking. "What? How?"

"Overdose, they say," he said.

"You're kidding," I said.

"It happens, even to somebody whose been clean for a long time. Doesn't take much to fall off."

I shook my head. "Coby goes missing, and now Thompson is dead."

"You seeing a connection?" Ira said.

"No," I said. "Doesn't mean there isn't one, though."

I drove back to the Cove thinking about Thompson, a guy who seemed like a good man, a recovering man, dead of the very thing he tried to kick. I was tired. Tired of thinking about death. I remembered something Kafka said, that the meaning of life is only that it stops. I wanted to punch Kafka in the face. But he's dead, too.

At my place I cooked a can of chili, tossed in chopped onions and grated cheddar, and chased it with beer. I searched the news on my phone and found a story about Thompson's death. Sticking out like a busted leg was a statement from a guy named Weston Elliott. "We have to face the fact that cultish, religious recovery systems are doing more harm than good."

I Googled the guy and landed on a website for something called The O'Hair Society. Sounded like a toupee company. In the "About" section it explained the outfit was named for a woman named Madalyn Murray O'Hair. The name was familiar to me. I remember my mom talking about her. She shook her head as she did. A little more research brought up the bio of O'Hair, a devout atheist who rose to prominence in the 1960s by suing Baltimore public schools for mandating Bible readings as part of the curriculum. The case eventually became *Abington School District v. Schempp*, which went to the United States Supreme Court. The Court held that Bible reading in public schools violated the U. S. Constitution.

Weston Elliott was listed as the president and co-founder of The O'Hair Society, and the author of *From Pastor to Pagan* and *Don't Pretend: A Free-Thinking Guide for Children*.

I've had my run-ins with atheists before. You can be a rational agnostic, but not a dogmatic atheist. To say that you know for certain there is no God just proves you don't know how to think.

Deeper research got me to a story from way back in the *Atlanta Journal-Constitution*. Elliott was involved in a nasty custody dispute with his ex-wife. She'd gotten a restraining order against him for threatening to kidnap their son, which Elliott said was to keep him from his mother's "dangerous religious zeal."

I felt like having a convo with this guy Elliott.

But that would have to wait.

Something I'm not good at.

I settled on my futon and read more of *Fahrenheit 451*. Bradbury's dystopian novel was reading more like a documentary of our time. People scared of thinking for themselves, because the government was watching. Choosing then to be empty husks, without thought, doing what they are told. And especially not reading books.

I remembered something Bradbury said, that he wasn't writing to predict the future, but to prevent it.

Nice try, Ray.

In the morning, I took my swim, came back, showered, shaved, started the coffee. I put on some Beethoven to get the blood pumping. Symphony Number 3, "Eroica." It was his ode to the ideals of courage and heroism, originally dedicated to Napoleon. But then the French general declared himself to be emperor. Ludwig van was so incensed that he scratched out Napoleon's name from the dedication page so hard he tore through the paper. But the "Eroica" was big, bold, and expanded the symphonic form in ways never before achieved. It was the start, as they say, of something big.

Which is what I needed.

I was in the kitchen and started more coffee dripping when I heard a knock at the screen door. I expected it to be C Dog.

It wasn't.

"Sophie."

"Hello there."

"I'm . . . gobsmacked."

"Are you going to invite me in?"

"Um, let me get rid of the dancing girls first."

"Don't worry," she said, opening the screen. "I'll do it."

In she came. "You're always surprising me," she said. "I thought I'd surprise you for a change."

"Mission accomplished," I said.

"I'm glad I caught you at home."

"What if I wasn't here?"

"It's a nice day," she said. "And there's the beach."

"Perfect," I said. "Want to toss the Frisbee?"

W e tossed. Sophie is a natural athlete, good enough to play volleyball for UCLA. We had a nice workout, then went out in the chop and did some body surfing.

Then sat on the sand soaking up vitamin D.

At one point, she picked up a fistful of sand and let it slowly trickle out.

"When I was little, my mom called this the sands of time," she said. "As you let it out, you're supposed to think of the good things you want in life."

"And what are you thinking of now?" I said.

She smiled. "There's a nice pair of shoes I've had my eye on."

"I'm going to kiss you for that," I said. "Maybe that'll change your mind."

"It's worth a try," she said.

"First things first," I said. "You need to know about something that happened downtown. A guy with a gun. I had to put the hurt on him. And I took the gun."

She looked at me a long moment. "Just another day at the office?"

"That's it."

She nodded. "You can go ahead and change my mind now."

The persuasion began.

W e spent an hour at my place, listening to jazz, talking. She had a meeting to go to, and I had business in Silver Lake. Before she left, we made plans for the next weekend.

But remember what Robert Burns said about the best laid plans of mice and men oft going awry? He could have written that about me.

I t was late afternoon when I got to Silver Lake.

Silver Lake is a gentrified, neo-bohemian neighborhood nestled between the 5 and 101 freeways to the east and west, and lolling in the shadow of the Griffith Park Observatory and Dodger Stadium to the north and south. It's favored by hipsters. Clad in Scotch flannel shirts and cropped linen pants, they could be seen razor scootering past Silver Lake itself, built as a reservoir in 1907, and named for the L.A. Water Commissioner, Herman Silver, who had once run (unsuccessfully) for mayor on a reform ticket. "The city should govern the saloons, instead of the saloons ruling the city," he said. How quaint.

The Caldwell for Mayor headquarters was in an office space between a Chinese restaurant and a Wells Fargo bank.

I went in and saw a few people at a few desks doing various things like talking on the phone and stuffing envelopes. The closest was a young woman, maybe mid-twenties, who was tapping away on a laptop. Her hair was spiked, with the colors sky blue and peach pink prominent. There was a clear portrait of a beautiful woman tattooed on her right forearm.

"Nice ink," I said.

She looked up and smiled. "Hi," she said.

"Who is it?" I said, pointing to her arm.

"Joan Jett," she said.

"I've heard of her," I said. "I Love Rock and Roll, right?"

She sang. "Put another dime in the jukebox, baby. I love rock and roll, come and take your time and dance with me."

"A classic," I said.

She looked at my left arm. "What's that say?"

"Vincit Omnia Veritas," I said. "Latin. It means truth conquers all things."

"That's weird," she said.

"It is?"

"I mean, what truth are you talking about?"

"Maybe there's something called *the* truth."

"That's really weird."

"Is it?"

"Sure," she said. "I mean, my truth is not necessarily your truth, right?"

"Plato and Aristotle would disagree," I said.

"Philosopher guys, yeah? But they're kind of old school."

"Some of us believe that school is still in session."

"Whoa. You talk kind of funny."

"I've been told that," I said. "So let's shift to this. If I wanted to talk to somebody here about Tatum Walker and Sonhouse, who would that be?"

She frowned. "Is this about Tommy Thompson?"

"No," I said.

"Do you know what happened?" she said.

"Yes."

"We're all just blown away."

"My questions have to do with somebody who was staying at Sonhouse," I said. "He's missing."

"Are you with the police?" she said.

"I work for a lawyer. We're representing the guy who's missing."

Her eyes suddenly got that look of suspicion that's as common as gridlock L.A. People don't trust anybody anymore, from congressmen to journalists to doctors to lawyers, right on down to that teenager holding her phone, ready to capture one wrong word you say so she can post it on Instagram.

To allay her fears I took out one of Ira's cards and handed it to her. "We're on the same side of this one," I said.

She looked at the card. "You know who you should talk to? Elijah Rowe. He's in charge of all our media."

"Is he here?"

She shook her head. "He left about half an hour ago. But you'll probably find him at The Den. He usually goes there after work. It's a cigar bar two blocks from here."

"How will I know him?"

"You'll know. He looks like Brad Pitt, only younger."

"Can I tell him you sent me?"

"I'm Corrine," she said. She put out her hand.

"Mike," I said shaking.

"Come back anytime, Mike," she said. "We can talk rock."

"And put dimes in a jukebox?"

"Come and take your time and dance with me," she said, and laughed.

. . .

T he Den was a retail tobacco shop with a lounge in the back. The lounge had exposed brick walls, an Edison bulb chandelier, and stuffed leather chairs. There was a small bar at the far end. A couple of the chairs were occupied by rotund gents chatting away, cigars in hand.

The only Brad Pitt lookalike was sitting alone. He had a Churchill size cigar in his mouth, a glass of amber liquid in one hand and his phone in the other. He wore a tight blue T-shirt over blue jeans, and low-gum sneakers. His feet were crossed and rested on the table in front of him.

"Elijah?" I said.

He looked up.

"Corrine sent me," I said.

He put his drink down on the arm of the chair, removed his cigar, and said, "Have a seat."

I sat.

"Join me?" he said, nodding to his glass.

"I'm good," I said.

"At least have a cigar."

"I'm in training," I said.

"I run 5Ks," he said.

"While smoking?"

He laughed. "Maybe I should try that. Be great pub. So what's up?"

"My name's Mike Romeo, I work for a lawyer named Ira Rosen. We rep a kid named Coby Keaton, who we got into Sonhouse. Only he walked out. We don't know where he is. I was told your campaign has an ear to the street."

"Who told you that?"

"A friend," I said.

He eyed me warily. "You're being a bit cryptic."

"Cryptic is a good word," I said. "From the Latin *crypticus*, meaning hidden."

Rowe took a contemplative puff on his cigar. "This conversation is taking a turn I didn't see coming."

"Happens to me all the time," I said.

"Look, I don't mean to be rude, but I don't know you. I don't know why I'm talking to you, or if I should."

"I've explained," I said.

"So you say," Rowe said. "But what people say and who they are are two different things these days, or can be."

"Like politicians?"

"Some," he said. "Not all."

"Duncan Caldwell?"

"The real deal," Rowe said. "What you see is what you get."

"I am, too," I said. I fished out an Ira card and handed it to him.

As he looked it over, an extra-large guy wearing a black T-shirt came over and said, "How you doing, Elijah?"

"Good," Rowe said. "Bring my friend a Macallan, neat."

"That's okay," I said.

"On the campaign," Rowe said. "Since this is business."

Extra Large nodded, and left.

"Reason I'm careful," Rowe said, "is somebody's threatening to expose Tatum Walker. We work closely with him. That's not going to look good."

"Expose him for what?"

"I shouldn't say any more."

"Why not?" I said.

"Last thing we need is some lawsuit," Rowe said.

"For what?"

"Defamation."

"You're talking to me," I said.

"There's ears everywhere," he said.

"You really are a careful fellow."

"Have to be." He paused. "Have I got your professional assurance this is confidential?"

"You've got my word."

"That used to mean something," Rowe said.

"To me it still does," I said.

"Okay. Your word. I'll hold you to it. Here it is. They're saying Tatum Walker talks a big game, family values, all that. He's got a wife and two kids, both grown. But they say he likes a little candy on the side."

"Is there any evidence of that?"

"They say they have a woman willing to talk."

"Who is they?"

"We don't know for sure. I've got my eye on the incumbent, but there are a lot of groups out there with money for dirty tricks.'"

"How about Weston Elliott?" I said.

Rowe's eyes widened. "You've done some homework."

"My job."

"Yeah," Rowe said. "He could be involved. He's got it in for Tatum, for sure."

Extra Large returned with a lowball glass on a fancy tray. I took it and said, "Thanks."

Rowe lifted his glass. "Your health."

We drank.

Rowe looked at his glass. "Warm bread and raisins, finishing notes of pear and peppery clove."

"Scotch," I said.

Rowe snorted. "You're a simple man, aren't you?"

"Not the adjective I would have chosen."

"We're in a delicate position," Rowe said. "There may be nothing to this. Maybe this is a ploy to get Tatum to make a public statement of denial, which brings it all out into the open. That puts us on the line, too. Even if the accusation proves to be bogus, it still carries a stigma. The masses don't seem to care whether something is true or not. They just see it on X, and that's that."

"Social media is the new opiate of the people," I said.

"Got that right," Rowe said. "And yet the reality is we've all got to use it. Right now our position is to say nothing."

"And hope it all goes away."

"A political campaign is all about hope," Rowe said.

"And an investigation is all about answers," I said. "Which brings me back to my client."

"What did you say his name was?"

"Coby Keaton." I described him and told Rowe a bit about the case.

"I can definitely make some calls," Rowe said.

"Appreciate it," I said. Out of courtesy, I hung a bit until I finished my drink. We talked about AI taking over the world. Rowe thought there'd always be a human element involved, and that was our hope. I averred there'd always be a human element involved, and that was our doom.

"I like that," Rowe said. "Can I quote you?"

"You can use it yourself," I said. "I prefer to stay anonymous."

"You know, we might be able to use a guy like you. You available?"

"Full plate," I said.

He nodded. "I'll be in touch if I hear anything."

"Thanks for the drink," I said.

The scotch had my tongue primed for meat. I drove over to Stout Burgers and Beer on Cahuenga and ordered their Mr. America with a side of tots, and a Heater Allen pilsner. The party in my mouth was just getting started when Ira called.

"Can you talk?" Ira said.

"Since I was six months old," I said.

"Will you ever stop?"

I said nothing.

"Perfect," Ira said. "I found out that someone named Trish Wilder rented a sedan from Eminence Luxury Rentals. There are several Trish or Patricia Wilders out there. One is a lawyer. Another works for an insurance company. Another is all over social media."

"Pictures?"

"The last one has an avatar of Carmen Miranda."

"The woman who followed me did not have fruit on her head," I said.

"I don't think this is a rabbit hole worth pursuing," Ira said. "On the other hand, the autopsy on Zon is. His name was Alonzo Perez. He was from San Diego, had a juvenile record there, sealed. He had 80cc's of meth in him. That dosage is large enough to kill a man who was not a regular user habituated to the drug."

"Tommy Thompson OD'd," I said.

"And?"

"What if Zon and Thompson got dosed by somebody else, who knew exactly what he was doing?"

"You mean murder?" Ira said.

"Just a thought," I said.

"A thin reed."

"Enough thin reeds can weave a basket," I said. I told him about my meeting with Elijah Rowe.

"Keep weaving," Ira said.

"You, too. And—wait a minute. Sophie's calling."

"Take it," Ira said.

.   .   .

"What's up?" I said.

Sophie said, "Mike, there's a guy outside my building. He keeps looking up at my window. I just thought—"

"Be there in twenty," I said.

I left the burger, tots, and beer and paid the bill.

It took me thirteen minutes to get to Sophie's.

There wasn't anybody on the street in front of her apartment building. I cruised up and down once to make sure. I parked. I announced myself at the entrance and Sophie buzzed me in. I took the stairs to the second floor.

She was standing at her open door. She had on a white sweater and blue jeans, and no shoes, like she was ready for a walk on the beach.

I took her hand. "You doing okay?"

"I'm fine," she said. "I just thought you should know. It's probably nothing."

"Or something," I said.

She closed the door. I went to her window that looked out on the street.

"Tell me where he was," I said.

Sophie came to the window and pulled the shade aside.

"About where your car is," she said. "I had the window open. I went to close it and looked down and saw him. He was just standing there, looking right up here. I closed the window, drew the curtains. I told myself it was nothing, that the guy was waiting for somebody, and just happened to look up at that moment. I waited maybe ten minutes, then went and peeked out. He was in the same spot. That's when I called you."

"Can you describe him? How was he dressed?"

"Latino, maybe thirties. A brown shirt, black pants. Nothing striking. I didn't linger."

"Was he next to a car?"

"No. Just standing on the sidewalk."

"Could be a random creep," I said.

"Plenty of those around," Sophie said.

"Or . . ."

"Or what?"

I hesitated. "Maybe he knows you and I are . . . whatever we are."

She took my hand then and led me to the sofa. She gave me a shove and I fell onto it. She sat and faced me, one leg folded under her.

"So what are we?" she said.

"That is the question," I said.

"You can't quote Shakespeare to get out of this," she said. "Wait here."

S he brought out a bottle of cabernet and we talked. For two hours we talked. I filled her in about the case, about Coby missing and Thompson dying. I even talked about boxing Diggs at Jimmy's.

That got us into sports. Sophie told me about growing up in San Diego, hitting her teens feeling ugly and gawky. Until she found volleyball and later became captain of her high school team.

I told her how I felt ugly and chunky, found philosophy and chess, and still felt ugly and chunky.

She knew about my parents being gunned down at Yale. And how that turned me from Michael Chamberlain into Mike Romeo.

Then somehow we got on the topic of our favorite movies, favorite foods, favorite books. We had a friendly argument over *The Great Gatsby*. She held it in high esteem. I said it should be replaced in high school reading lists with *The Maltese Falcon*, which has greed, desire, deception, and murder. And a man's duty in his profession.

"That's you," Sophie said.

"Me?"

"You're Sam Spade."

"Doesn't that make you Brigid O'Shaughnessy?"

"Oh, thank you," she said.

"I didn't mean to imply that you're a pathological liar, I just—"

"The hole is just getting bigger, Romeo. Stop digging."

We kept talking. And then she was in my arms, her head resting on me just below the shoulder. I was telling her about Penelope, wife of Odysseus, who was off fighting the Trojans. Suitors kept coming for her, insisting Odysseus was dead, demanding she marry one of them. She said she first had to finish weaving a shroud for Odysseus' old man, Laertes. At night, she'd secretly unravel what she had woven that day. Clever wife.

Sophie said nothing because she was asleep.

I listened to her breathe. And started to breathe with her, same rhythm, my chest rising and falling like a boat in a quiet harbor, anchored.

Yeah. Waiting for the storm.

I lifted her and carried her to the bedroom. She made soft noises as I put her on the bed and covered her with the throw blanket. I turned out the lights.

I went back to the window and looked out and wondered if it had been just some guy or somebody targeting Sophie to get to me. Was that the way it would always be? Yeah, obviously, that was the whole matter in a nutshell.

Then again, nobody's safe. The world hangs anvils over our heads, held by fraying ropes. Try to avoid one and you'll walk under another. You either curl up in a corner and stay there, or you go out and make your best move, day by day, just like I told C Dog.

I went to the bedroom and looked at Sophie's face. Peaceful. Beautiful.

Safe. At least for the moment.

Then back to the living room. I shut off the lights and stretched out on the sofa. For maybe half an hour I asked myself what words I should say to Sophie when we spoke next.

And then I fell asleep.

I woke up to dim morning light and the smell of coffee brewing.

"Black, please," I said.

"Good morning," Sophie said from the kitchen. She came to the living room. She wore a fresh blue sweatshirt over gray, loose-flowing pants.

"I conked out," I said, sitting up.

"No charge," she said. "I'll make us some breakfast."

"Sounds good."

She turned.

"Wait," I said.

She turned back.

"There's something I want to say."

"Intriguing," she said.

"Have a seat."

"Even more intriguing." She sat next to me.

"Ever read The Razor's Edge?" I asked.

"By Maugham? No, but I saw the Tyrone Power movie in a college film class."

"Maugham took his title from a Hindu Upanishad. The sharp edge of a razor is difficult to pass over, thus sayeth the wise, the path to salvation is hard."

"Is that what you wanted to say?"

"I'm just warming up. You'll recall that it's about Larry

Darrell, who gets back from World War I and can't look at the world the same way again. His circle, including his fiancée, are going on with life just like before. He can't do that. Can't take the easy way. The war changed him. He goes off to Paris where a lot of American expatriates are, looking for something, something deeper, something with ultimate meaning. His fiancée can't wait any longer and marries a rich guy."

"Isn't there a character in it named Sophie who doesn't end up so well?"

"If you mean drug addiction, alcoholism and promiscuity, then yes."

"I'm not sure I like where this is going."

"Hang in there. The name is just a coincidence. The point is Larry is living on the razor's edge, searching for salvation. I can relate, only my razor is one of those five-blade deals. I keep looking at my steps, my moves. Well, there's one step I need to take now."

I took a deep breath, then took her hand. "I want you with me, from now on, forever."

Her hand trembled.

"It's a hard ask, I know," I said. "But I'm asking."

For a long moment she said nothing. That silence was like a held breath, a hush at the edge of a cliff.

Slowly, she pulled my hand to her cheek and closed her eyes.

"I'll walk the edge with you," she said. "All the way."

As I drove back to the Cove, back home, I felt something strange for me—elation. I was somewhere up in the sky riding a racehorse, heading into the stretch, maybe I could actually make it to the finish line because sometime soon going home would mean going home to her. There was optimism, too, another stranger, believing now that the world

could make sense to two people huddled together against the
storm. Yet right behind it, too, a fear, a pondering of all the
ways I could bring the hurt, and all of a sudden I was
screaming out loud, "Shut up! Don't blow it, you stupid
idiot!"

It was foggy along the coast, and I thought of that book by
the anonymous Christian mystic, The Cloud of Unknowing,
which is what I was driving through, in my car and in my
mind. My mom taught that book at Yale Divinity, and once
tried to explain it to me, how it was a prayer of reaching out in
love, not intellect, an opening of the heart and allowing yourself to be naked before grace and to rest in the dark awareness
of trust. It didn't make sense to me then, but started to now
because of Sophie, and when I pulled in at my place I was
laughing and crying at the same time.

I dove into the work to be finished. I looked again at the
legal memo Ira prepared after Coby's arraignment. There
was nothing in it to indicate where Coby might have gone. He
had no connections in L.A., except Zon.

But he did have that sister in Las Vegas. Ira had put down
her phone number. I called it. Got voicemail.

"My name is Mike Romeo, I work for a lawyer named Ira
Rosen. We're representing your brother. He's in trouble. Can
we talk about it?"

She called back five minutes later.

"It's Pamela Keaton," she said.

"Thanks for calling," I said.

"What trouble is he in?"

"He got attacked by a guy high on meth and had to defend
himself. He ended up killing the man."

"Dear God."

"It was clearly self-defense," I said. "We placed him in a

recovery program, but he skipped out. He hasn't contacted you, has he?"

"No."

"If he does, try to find out where he is and let me know, will you?"

"Are you really representing him?"

"You can Google Ira Rosen and you'll find out he's legit," I said.

She paused. "Have you talked to Brad Skinner?"

Memory jog. Coby had mentioned his name at our first interview. He was the high school friend Coby had stayed with when he first got to L.A.

I said, "Would you happen to have his contact information?"

"I don't," she said. "But Coby told me he lived in… wait… um, a park. Liner Park, something like that."

"Pamela, if anything else occurs to you, don't hesitate to call me."

"Is he going to be okay?"

"We've got to find him first," I said.

"Please find him," she said. It sounded like she was crying.

I Googled "Liner Park Los Angeles" and got a few hits on places with "Linear Park" in the name. Actual parks, but labeled linear because they're longer than they are wide.

I tried "Limer Park." Google showed results for "Leimert Park." A neighborhood south of the 10 freeway.

I called Ira and told him about my talk with Pamela Keaton, and asked if he could find a Brad Skinner in Leimert Park. He told me to hang on. I heard him tapping his keyboard.

"Leimert Park is where they found the Black Dahlia," he said. *Tap tap tap.* "Here we go. A last known address for a Brad Skinner." He gave it to me.

"I'll check it out," I said. "And see if you can set up a meeting for me with Tatum Walker. If I'm going to drive all over town I might as well string poop."

"What did you just say?"

"It's an expression Joey Feint used to use. Meant putting ordinary tasks together. Only he didn't use the word poop."

"Precious," Ira said.

I t took me an hour in traffic to get over to Leimert Park. It was old-school L.A., lots of houses that had been built in the 1920s and 30s. Apartment buildings dotted around, but even they gave the impression they were out of breath and ready to give up the ghost.

The one where Brad Skinner was supposed to live had an outside gate and a courtyard. The apartment was number four on the ground level. The courtyard once had grass, but now was jigsaw puzzle pieces of dirt patches. A kid's bike lay on its side next to a soccer ball. No kids in sight.

I knocked on the door. Got nothing. Knocked again. Nada.

Stringing poop.

I went to number three and knocked. A woman's voice behind the door said, "Who is it?"

"I'm Looking for Brad Skinner," I said.

"Doesn't live here no more," she said.

"He moved?"

"Yeah."

"You know where?"

"No."

"Can I ask you something?"

"What."

"Can you open the door?"

"I don't know who you are."

"A friend of a friend of his," I said. "I wonder if you might have seen this friend?" I took out a postcard-sized print of Coby's mug shot and held it up to the peep hole.

Pause.

"Oh yeah, a couple years ago," she said. "Haven't seen him since. Cory or something."

"Coby," I said "I work for his lawyer."

"His lawyer?"

"Can I give you our card?"

The door opened a crack. It had a chain on it. The woman's face looked ten years older than she probably was. I handed her the card.

"I don't know if he'll show up," I said. "But if you see him, tell him Mike was here looking for him."

"I guess I can do that," she said. "He was a funny guy."

"Thanks," I said.

She closed the door.

As I walked out I saw a guy sitting—wedged, actually—in the corner of the fence that went around the building. He wore grimy clothes, had a matted beard and a dirty, gargoyle face. He didn't move, but his eyes locked on me. I wondered why I hadn't seen him when I came in. His look and smell were hard to miss.

As I opened the gate, his low, guttural voice said, "Your mother's in hell."

I whipped around at him. He was smiling.

"She's waiting for you," he said.

Fire flared in me, all of me, burning away all thought. I was half a second away from kicking his face. There's a pit in my gut because my mom was cut down in the prime of her life, and this guy had just poured acid in the pit. I almost threw up. That's what saved him.

But it didn't save me. There it was, Romeo's fire, the thing I can't control, the thing that makes me unfit for normality, for home and hearth and picket fences. When I'm this way, I have to get away from people, any and all. I stumbled away and got in Spinoza, my hands shaking.

I took off and drove the streets, not caring which ones, not knowing which way, trying to let the fire die down. Why did he say that? My mother's face was in my mind now, alive and smiling, putting a cold cloth on my head when I was sick.

Why why why?

I stopped by a liquor store and hit my dashboard a few times. Then stroked it and said to my car, "I'm sorry, old boy, you didn't deserve that."

I sat there for maybe half an hour, watching people go in and out of the liquor store. How many of them used booze to douse their own flames? Or make them flare up into domestic violence, drunk driving, or singing on a street corner?

Finally, I was calm enough to drive to Sonhouse.

Tatum Walker was at his desk working on his laptop.

"Mike," he said. "Good to—"

"Can we talk?"

"Sure, can you give me—"

"Sooner the better," I said.

He nodded, closed the laptop. "What is it, Mike?"

"What's going on here? How could you let Thompson overdose?" It was unfair. But I wasn't feeling fair. I was feeling fire.

"Whoa, Mike," Walker said. "Where is this coming from?"

"You have an answer or not?"

"With something like this," Walker said, "there can be a million whys, and a bunch of them can get all tangled up together. Nobody saw this coming. We're still in shock, can you understand that?"

I plopped in a chair.

"What's wrong, Mike?"

I took a deep breath and told him about the guy at the apartment in Leimert Park. I told him about my mom and dad getting gunned down and how that chewed me up.

My chest was tight when I finished.

Walker said, "I'm gonna tell you something, Mike. Might be a tester for you. But here it is. That sounds like a demon."

I frowned. "You're saying you think that guy was actually a demon?"

"No. A demon inside him. That happens, you know."

"I don't know," I said.

"Demonic possession is a real thing, Mike. And it seems to be happening more and more. Think about it. That demon knew about you. And he knew what to say to get to you. He knew your mom was dead. Demons have that kind of knowledge. But then he said your mom was in hell. That hit you in the gut, right?"

"Yeah, it did."

"They know where you're vulnerable," Walker said. "But you have to know something else. Demons lie. They lie when it suits their purposes, which are deception, madness, and death."

I said, "Why would a demon bother with me?"

"Because you're an honest man, seeking the truth. That's what it says on your arm, right? Demons want to keep people from the truth, which is found right here."

Tatum Walker lifted a worn Bible from his desk and held it up. "My granddaddy gave me this Bible when I got out of prison. Told me to read up or shut up."

"I need to tell you something," I said.

He placed the Bible back on the desk. "Go for it."

"There's somebody out there about to plant an unflattering story about you."

His eyes narrowed. "Wouldn't be the first time. You know what it's about?"

"I'll give it to you straight. Extra-marital activity."

Walker's shoulders drooped. He shook his head. "My family. Don't mess with my family. Who is it?"

"I don't know," I said. "I got the information secondhand."

Tatum Walker's expression changed to ice. "Who is the hand?"

"Unfortunately, I can't say because it was given to me in confidence."

He waited a long time before answering. "Okay, I respect that. Now hear me out. I've been lied about for a long time. It goes with the territory. Anybody serving the Lord in a public way gets it. Jesus was lied about. His apostles were, too."

"I'm sorry I brought it up."

"I don't blame you. You want to know if you can trust me, considering what happened to Zon and Coby. You're just doing your job."

"You're being charitable," I said.

"He that is without sin among you, let him cast the first stone."

"Maybe I can find out who's throwing the rocks."

"Find Coby instead," Walker said. "That's who counts right now."

As I was walking out I saw Nathan White, Thompson's assistant, sitting alone at a table by a window. His head rested on one hand as he stared out. I walked over.

"Pretty rough," I said.

That startled him. "What? Oh. Yeah."

I sat on the bench next to him. "Who found him?"

He was about to speak, but the words stuck in his throat.

"Did you have any idea he might have fallen off the wagon?" I said.

Nathan White thought about it. "I know he had a son somewhere. Used to talk to me about him sometimes. How he was missing out on his life because he lived with his mother in . . . I think it's Idaho."

"Or who might have supplied him?" I said.

"Nobody here," White said. "He was doing so good."

"What do you know about a guy named Weston Elliott?"

"Him? He's a gasbag. Pardon my French."

"Your French is fine," I said. "Anything else you can tell me?"

"He makes a lot of noise," Nathan said. "Other than that…" His voice trailed off with a tremble.

I put my hand on his shoulder. "Maybe you should go home."

He shook his head. "Too much to do."

"It's okay to take a break," I said. "I'm sure Reverend Walker would understand."

Nathan took a deep breath. "Why does God take the good ones?"

I paused a moment. "It's the oldest question, isn't it?"

"It is?"

"Why do the righteous suffer? Job's question. Why do they die before their time?"

"Yeah," Nathan said. "So what's the answer?"

"Philosophers and theologians have been working on that for four thousand years."

"Have you worked on it?"

"Oh yeah. You can't really live without thinking about it. And maybe that's part of the answer."

"What is?"

"The thinking. It keeps us awake, keeps us contemplating what's just and unjust."

"I just don't want it to hurt anymore," Nathan said.

"Give it time."

"Time heals all wounds, huh?"

"It also wounds all heels."

Nathan frowned, then a little smile came to his face. I counted it a small victory.

W ith nothing else doing, I drove around downtown. Maybe I'd see Coby walking around. Or Bigfoot having a street taco. Or a unicorn grazing in Pershing Square.

Tent communities were everywhere. The city had been trying out a program to clear encampments, put the people into hotels, and then find them permanent housing. But that hasn't been easy, and the funds to pay for the hotel rooms were running thin.

Many end up going right back to the street.

I covered the ground between Main and Broadway, from Sixth all the way to Temple. It got slow on First because of a pro-Palestinian protest gaggle in front of the L.A. Law Library. A big banner announcing "From the River to the Sea, Palestine Will Be Free" rippled in angry hands.

Up at the Superior Courthouse, suited lawyers walked in and out with phones stuck to their ears, ignoring the guy in a wheelchair with an American flag on it, holding out a cup.

I turned left on Grand and drove past the Disney Concert Hall and The Broad art museum, which looks like a cinder block on a tilt. Down the hill and into the flats, I started feeling like Coronado searching Mexico for the Seven Cities of Gold. I finally had enough. Maybe Coby wasn't even in L.A. anymore. Maybe he was lying dead behind a dumpster.

Maybe it was time to call it quits on the whole thing.

But quit doesn't sit well with me.

. . .

I drove to Jimmy's and worked the heavy bag for awhile, jumped some rope. Jeremiah Diggs showed up and we danced a little, with Jimmy in the ring showing us footwork.

After, I said I was going to grab a Tommy burger. Diggs asked me what a Tommy burger was.

"It cannot be explained," I said. "It must be experienced."

"He's in training," Jimmy said.

"Be quiet," I said.

Diggs and I walked to Tommy's on Topanga. There I introduced him to chili-laden happiness in a bun. His reaction was ecstatic. It was a beautiful thing. My day's work was done.

Next morning I drove to Eminence Luxury Rentals. It was in a tony building at the west end of the Sunset Strip. The office was pink and blue and smelled of lavender. A woman at the front desk was dressed to the eights, the nines being reserved for night life.

She smiled. Her perfect white teeth reflected the light. "May I help you?" she said.

"Interested in a rental," I said. "Trish Wilder sent me."

The smile intensified. "Trish? Fantastic." She stood and extended her hand. "I'm Rosemary."

"Mike."

We shook. Hers was a confident, you'll-be-glad-you-did-business-with-me grip.

"You've come to the right place," she said.

"I'll bet you say that to all the renters," I said.

"Only the rich, handsome ones," she said.

"I really am in the right place."

She issued an appreciative laugh. "What sort of ride are you looking for?"

"Well, you know, Trish and I are on the same team."

"You work for the campaign?"

"Of course," I said. "And just between you and me, I'm always interested in what the good citizens of our fair city are thinking. You have any thoughts on how we're running things?"

"I don't follow politics. But the polls seem to be favorable. And looks are pretty important these days."

"Tell me what you mean by that," I said.

"It's obvious, isn't it? Duncan Caldwell looks the part. He's another Newsom. That'll take him a long way."

"Must be the hair," I said.

"So what date did you have in mind?" she said.

"Hold on." I took out my phone and looked at the home screen. I frowned. "Well, that doesn't make sense."

"What doesn't?" she said.

"Let me make a quick call."

"Of course," Rosemary said. "Can I get you a cappuccino?"

"I'm good," I said. I turned and strolled back toward the door. I put the phone to my ear and said to nobody, "Hey, it's Mike. I'm down here at Eminence. What was the date again? It's not on my calendar… uh huh… what? You're kidding. I'm here now… why?… come on…all right, all right. I'll be right over."

I stuck the phone back in my pocket. "Change of plans," I said. "I swear, sometimes the left hand doesn't know where the right hand is hanging out."

"That's too bad," Rosemary said.

"Another time," I said.

"I hope so," she said.

· · ·

I drove through the In-N-Out on Sunset near LaBrea. Ordered a double-double, animal style, with fries and a Coke. This was going to cost me a long swim and wind sprints on the beach, but it was worth it. I parked across the street from Hollywood High School. The place still had the feel of old Hollywood, like when Judy Garland was around. The towering palm trees were definitely over a hundred years old. They looked tired, like they wanted to tell the current crop of students to get off the lawn.

Some of those students were milling around in front of the stairs, backpack slung over shoulders, virtually all of them looking at phones. The future of America being trained by TikTok how to live life in ten-second bites.

I called Ira.

"We need to focus on Duncan Caldwell," I said.

"Why is that?" Ira said.

"I went to Eminence Rentals. Found out Trish Wilder, that woman who followed me, was doing work for the Caldwell campaign. I want to know what's going on. What's his interest in Sonhouse? Why is he having people followed?"

"I have a question for you," Ira said. "What does this have to do with finding our client?"

"Maybe there's a connection."

"What connection?"

"I said maybe. And anyway, I don't have any other leads. Coby could be anywhere. Or dead."

"Steady, boy. Where are you now?"

"Fancy luncheon, Hollywood."

"Which drive-thru?"

"In-N-Out."

"Come on over."

"I don't think so," I said.

"Michael, don't get too lone wolf on me."

"If I get trapped, can I at least chew my own leg off?"

"Michael—"

"Goodbye, Ira."

I ate the last of my fries on the way to Caldwell headquarters in Silver Lake. Corrine, the Joan Jett fan, was the only one there.

"Hiya, Mike!" she said.

"Where is everybody?" I said.

"The press conference. Starts in an hour."

"Why aren't you there?"

"Somebody has to hold down the fort," she said.

"Interesting metaphor."

"Huh?"

"Depends on the fort," I said. "You know the story of the Alamo?"

"The movie theater?"

"The fort."

"There's a fort?"

"In Texas."

"Cool."

"Everybody in it died," I said.

"Uncool," she said. "When did that happen?"

"1836."

"Whoa. That is, like, a long time ago."

I said, "Do you know how I can get in touch with Trish Wilder?"

"Who?"

"Trish Wilder. She works with the campaign."

Corrine's brow furrowed in thought. She opened a drawer and pulled out some papers stapled together. It was a list of names. She flipped to the last page and scanned it.

"I don't see that name here," she said. "You sure she works for us?"

"Not really," I said. "It was just a shot."

"Who is she?"

"I don't know that, either."

"Is this some sort of fishing trip?" she said.

"I guess it is."

"Maybe," she said, "you're fishing in the wrong stream." She blinked her eyes a few times.

I cleared my throat. "Corrine, I should let you know, my fishing days are over."

"You seeing someone?"

"More than that."

"You're married?"

"Not yet."

"Man."

"What?"

She shook her head. "Not any marriable guys out there."

"You want to get married?" I said.

"I think about it."

"It's a good thought," I said. "Keep having it. You never know."

Corrine said nothing.

"Maybe I can make the press conference," I said. "Where is it?"

Venice is a beachfront neighborhood a little south of Santa Monica. It opened in 1905, developed by a tobacco millionaire named Abbot Kinney. He modeled it after the canals in the real Venice, and made it a pleasure attraction. There was a mini-railroad, a dance hall, a boardwalk. There was also a freak show, which was a picture of things to come.

After World War II, the place was run down, with a lot of

the canals covered with cement. It became a Bohemian hangout full of beatniks, street performers, artists, vendors of various sorts. And Muscle Beach, where bodybuilders preened in tight swimsuits to the ogling pleasure of the female contingent.

Now it was a mix of wealthy homeowners and down-and-outers. Making it the perfect place for a mayoral candidate to wax eloquent on the need for a cleaner, safer city.

When I got there and managed to find a parking spot, I had to walk five blocks to get within shouting distance of the spot, which was cordoned off by a combination of police barriers and security guards.

Approaching, I saw one of the guards going jaw to jaw with what looked like a member of what is euphemistically called "the housing-deprived community."

"Sir, you cannot," the guard said. "I'm telling you, you cannot."

"Beenherelonger'nyou," the other responded, then issued a string of epithets that would have made a Brooklyn stevedore blush.

"Sir...sir..." the guard said, hands up as if to protect himself.

What sounded like *mutterbuckerbucketmutterbucket* issued forth from the anxious interloper.

I passed by the enlightened colloquy and found a place outside the tape where I could see the temporary dais and a podium with a *Caldwell for Mayor* sign on it. At the podium was a woman who I recognized from the headquarters.

"...will be provided to you," she was saying. "Any follow-up questions can come directly to me. All your inquiries will be answered. So without further delay, let me introduce the next mayor of Los Angeles, Duncan Caldwell!"

No applause.

Caldwell, smiling like a summer's day, stepped up to the

podium. He wore an open-neck shirt. A man of the people would never wear a tie in such a venue.

"Welcome, everyone," Caldwell said. "It's a great day here in Venice, and it's going to be a great new day in Los Angeles. But there are challenges. We have the largest homeless population of any city in the country. It is not being addressed effectively, and the responsibility rests squarely with City Hall. We have to understand something. The main cause of homelessness is not mental health or drug abuse or even poverty. It's a stereotype to think everybody that is unhoused has a mental health issue. Sure, there's a percentage that do. But let me just tell you something. If I was on the street long enough, I'd have a mental health or substance abuse issue, too."

Pause for dramatic effect.

"No, the primary cause is the cost and availability of housing. Under current leadership, our city is falling short of its housing production goals by about sixty percent, and only has one shelter bed for every three unhoused people. As mayor, I will require city agencies to report to the city council every three months on actual steps taken to address the homelessness crisis. I will suspend competitive bidding requirements for contracts related to the homelessness problem. And I will redirect city employees from any department toward work on the crisis."

I probably wasn't going to get through to the candidate this way. But there was someone up there I might be able to collar —my cigar-loving pal, Elijah Rowe. He was standing next to a guy with an iPhone on a stick, directing him. No doubt making a promo video.

I moved closer to the outer ring, catching the eye of a cop. I smiled at him. He did not smile back.

And then I saw Trish Wilder.

. . .

She was standing next to a security guard, her back to me, listening to the speech.

I tapped her shoulder.

"Tag," I said.

She spun around so fast she made a breeze. Her eyes popped. "What are you doing here?" she said.

"Came to see the show," I said. "Can we talk?"

"No," she said, clearly rattled.

The security guard, built like a bank vault door, said to Trish, "There a problem here?"

"No problem," Trish said. "He was just leaving."

"I was thinking of starting a fight with Bruno here," I said. "Take attention away from the candidate, generate a headline like Violence Breaks Out at Caldwell Presser."

Bruno looked like he wanted to throw the first punch.

"It's okay," Trish said. "Give us a minute."

She walked away.

"Another time," I said to Bruno.

"Anytime, chump," he said.

I joined Trish.

"What is it you want?" she said.

"I want to know why you were following me," I said.

"How did you find me?"

"It's what I do."

"Well you can undo it," she said. "I have nothing to say to you."

"So you work security for the Caldwell campaign," I said. "What's that got to do with me?"

"Nothing."

"Then why follow me?"

She shook her head.

"Trish," I said, "I'm not one to make it hard on anybody."

"Ha."

"Just tell me why you're so interested in me. I'm really charming once you get to know me."

A hint of a smile came to her face. She beat it back.

"Look" she said. "I saw you at Sonhouse and you stuck out like a sore thumb."

"That's a cliché," I said. "Can't I stick out like a side of beef?"

"I just wanted to know what you were about," she said. "I followed you when you left the place. I was observing activity from across the street."

"Why, exactly, were you observing?"

"You're representing a young man who was diverted to Sonhouse, but is missing now, right?"

"You know this how?"

"I looked up Ira Rosen. I know he's well regarded."

"Doing your homework," I said.

"That's what I do," she said. "Now, I have a question for you."

"You may approach."

"Did your client ever mention the name Lucifer to you?"

"Interesting," I said.

"That's not an answer," she said.

"But it is interesting," I said. "You know what he's charged with?"

"He killed someone who'd been with Sonhouse, who went by the name Zon."

"Zon was shouting 'Lucifer is coming' when the killing went down."

She chewed on that a moment. "So a guy high on meth shouts 'Lucifer.' What do you think that means?"

"How do you know he was high on meth?"

Pause. "His behavior sounded like a drug thing," she said.

"Trish, sometimes I think you're not being completely honest with me."

Her face hardened. "I don't really care what you think."

"Now you're just being unfriendly."

"I'm going back to work now," she said. "Excuse me."

She started to walk by me. I put my hand on her arm.

"Don't touch me," she said.

"We have more to talk about," I said.

"We do not."

Appearing like a ghost was Bruno. "There a problem here?"

"No," Trish said, walking away.

"You're done here," Bruno said to me.

"I'm a member of the public," I said. "Here to listen to a candidate for public office. Got a problem with that?"

"I got a problem with you," he said.

"Solve it," I said.

He clenched his hands.

"Let it go, Trag," Trish Wilder said.

"Your master calls," I said.

"Someday," he said.

"Noli velle quod non intelligis," I said.

His confused look was precious.

"Do not wish for what you do not understand," I said.

C aldwell finished his talk and took some questions. By the time things broke up, I was all the way around to the other end of the cordon. The candidate disappeared into the back of a black sedan. The sedan disappeared into the streets of Venice.

Elijah Rowe was getting ready to disappear.

I caught up with him.

"Elijah," I said.

He turned. Looked surprised, and not in a good way. "What are you doing here?"

"Deciding who to vote for," I said.

That brought out his professional smile. "No brainer," he said.

"And I was wondering, were you able to make any calls on that thing we talked about?"

"What thing?"

"Finding my client."

"Oh yeah, yeah. No. I've been kind of busy, as you can see."

"Any bone you can throw me I'd appreciate."

"Yeah, yeah. Let me make a note."

He took out his phone and double-thumbed it.

"Listen," he said. "Gotta run. I'll see what I can do."

"I'll buy you a cigar."

"Now you're talking," he said.

I drove to Ira's.

When I walked in, I said, "The wolf has returned."

Ira was in his wheelchair, a book on his lap. "No kills?" he said.

"I just gnawed a few people."

He nodded in his rabbinical way, but said nothing.

Then I told him about the Caldwell rally. But I spent more time talking about the guy who said my mom was in hell, because it was still bothering me. I told him what Tatum Walker said about demons. I finished by asking Ira, "Do you believe in a literal devil?"

"Of course," Ira said. He held up the book on his lap. It was the Hebrew scriptures. "He is the adversary, the accuser."

"What's he look like?"

"Well, he's not a guy with horns and a pitchfork dressed in red pajamas. I have a feeling he doesn't mind a bit if that's how he's portrayed. Makes it easy to hide in plain sight."

Ira's landline rang. The one he uses for lawyer business.

He started talking to someone, so I went to the backyard and stretched out on the grass under Ira's magnolia tree. This is my oasis—a spot of peace and quiet in the urban jungle. Sometimes I read here. Sometimes I just lie there with my hands behind my head and try to take a break from thinking. I tried that, and of course thought of many things

Sophie. Coby. Caldwell. Trish Wilder. The Joan Jett girl. The devil.

Sophie again. I let that thought linger. It was warm like the sun.

I started to doze, then heard Ira from the back door.

"Michael, come in here!"

I gave my head a good shake and went to him.

"What is it?" I said.

"Tatum Walker's in the hospital," he said. "Somebody tried to kill him."

It took us twenty minutes to get to the hospital. I pushed Ira's wheelchair from the parking structure through the labyrinthian hallways, getting to the desk where we got visitor badges. Then another journey till we found the emergency room.

We had to wait in line. At the window, Ira gave them his card and told them why we were here.

We were told to wait.

The waiting area was half filled with people in various stages of trauma, or with faces of concern as they waited for loved ones. There was a chair and a space for Ira's wheelchair near the door. But I couldn't sit for long. I got up and paced.

"Michael, sit," Ira said.

"I can't," I said.

"Try."

"I'll be back."

I left the room and started wandering the halls, rambling thoughts bouncing around. How could this have happened? *Why* had it happened? Who wanted Tatum Walker dead? Not just silenced, but deep-sixed? And what did the cops know, if anything?

Thompson dead, and Walker almost. The only connection with Coby Keaton was that Coby went missing before all this went down. A thin thread, yes. But spiders use them to spin webs.

I was half a block away when I got a text from Ira.

A detective wants to talk to us.

His name was Meyer, from Central Division. He was around fifty or so, with only a slight paunch. You used to tell the ages of cops by their paunches, like rings on a tree. Meyer kept himself in shape and had a springy energy to him. I sat in the chair next to Ira, Meyer stayed on his feet.

Ira said, "I've explained to Detective Meyer about our representation of Coby, and how he was at Sonhouse, and that's our connection with Tatum Walker. He wants to know if we should consider Coby a suspect. I said absolutely not."

"Do you agree with that?" Meyer asked me.

"I do," I said.

"Except that your client killed a man with a knife," Meyer said.

"That was self-defense," I said. "He's no killer."

"You understand why I'm asking," Meyer said.

"Sure," I said.

"Do you have any idea who might have a reason to want Tatum Walker dead?"

"He has enemies," I said.

"Any names?"

"It's pretty well known a guy named Weston Elliott has been tearing him down."

"Elliott?" Meyer tapped a note on his phone.

"A vocal atheist," I said.

"Anyone else?" Meyer asked.

"It could be random," I said. "It's not the greatest location down there."

"You don't have to tell me that," Meyer said.

Ira said, "Do you know any details of the attack?"

"There's a passageway outside the building," Meyer said. "That's where he was found."

"Who found him?" I said.

"Guy named Milo," Meyer said.

"I met him once," I said. "He a suspect?"

"Still an open question," Meyer said. "What can you tell me about him?"

"Not much," I said. "He likes chess."

Meyer nodded. "Anyone else?"

I said, "Sonhouse is full of addicts trying to get clean. Maybe somebody snapped."

Somebody screamed.

It was a woman on the other side of the waiting room. A security guard moved like lightning to see what the matter was.

"Nobody talking!" the woman said. "Nobody talking!"

The guard tried to calm her down. She wouldn't be calmed. She unleashed a string of expletives. Another guard went over.

"Ma'am, be quiet," he said. "Or we'll ask you to leave."

Meyer said, "Would you mind coming down tomorrow, give us a statement? This isn't the place for it."

"He'll be there," Ira said. He exchanged cards with Meyer.

The woman screamed again, and colorful language followed. The two guards lifted her out of her chair and started dragging her out.

She wailed. "Get your hands off me! Don't you touch me! Get your hands off!"

The guards got her outside. The waiting room went back to its regularly scheduled boredom.

"Just another fine day in L.A.," I said.

Meyer grunted, then went to the reception window. He got buzzed inside. Ten minutes later he came out and told us that Tatum was in critical but stable condition. He handed me his card.

"Tomorrow, then?" he said.

"He'll be there," Ira said.

I t took us fifteen minutes to wind our way back to Ira's van, and a full hour fighting traffic to get back to his house. I decided to spend the night so it wouldn't be as much of a ride to Central the next day.

Ira started making us dinner.

I went out back and called Sophie.

"A lot's been happening," I said.

"Of course," she said. "What can you tell me?"

"Why don't we just have a code word. MOS. More of the same."

"That would save time," Sophie said.

"Exactly."

"It would also be extremely unsatisfying."

"Somebody tried to kill Tatum Walker," I said. "Cut his throat."

"Oh no . . . "

"Yeah. Ira and I just went to the hospital. We didn't get to see him. He's critical but stable. Talked to a detective."

"Do they know who did it?"

"He thinks it may be Coby."

"Is that possible?"

"I don't think so," I said. "Then again, anything's possible. They're training cows in Germany to use a toilet."

"Very funny."

"True, actually. They call it a MooLoo."

"Why would they do that?" Sophie said.

"So our future steaks won't befoul the air, thus saving the Earth," I said.

"You've got be kidding."

"I don't kid about steaks," I said. "You and I will have one soon."

"I'll hold you to that," Sophie said.

After dinner Ira and I played a game of chess. This time I hit him with an old classic, the Pillsbury Attack, named for the American chess genius Harry Nelson Pillsbury, who introduced it in 1898. It rocked Ira and he had to scramble to get even. But he got there, and we agreed to a draw after thirty-five moves.

Ira went to bed and I sat up for awhile. I tried to read some, but kept thinking how this whole Coby mess could end in a draw. We might never find him. Tatum's would-be killer might get away. The police files are filled with unsolveds. Life would go on. But I'd always be thinking of moves I should have made, that I missed something I should have seen.

Around eleven I went to bed, but didn't fall asleep for a long time.

At nine the next morning, I called Central Division. Meyer was in. It took me forty-five minutes to get there via Wilshire. They had my name on a list and let me park in their lot.

I checked in at the front. Meyer came out to get me, took me inside to an interview room.

"Thanks for coming," he said. "I'll take your statement, we'll transcribe it right here, and you can look it over and sign it. Shouldn't take too long."

"I've got all day."

"And you'd just love to spend it with the cops, right?" Meyer laughed.

"Some of my best friends are cops," I said.

"Oh yeah? Who?"

"Coltrane Smith."

"Cole? How do you know him?"

"We've had some mutual interests of a legal nature," I said.

"Great guy," Meyer said. "Says he might go private."

"I've heard that."

"Sam Spade," Meyer said. "Like you."

"I'm more of a Philip Marlowe man," I said.

"Okay, Phil." He smiled, picked up a pencil and tapped it on the desk. "Let me ask you a question, if I may."

"Sure."

"Monday night, around ten. Where were you?"

There was the slightest change in his face. A tensing of the jaw muscles.

"Interesting," I said. "That's something you ask a suspect."

"It's also something we ask to eliminate people," Meyer said.

"Routine?"

"Routine."

"I get it," I said. I thought for a moment. "I was at home."

"Where is that?"

"Paradise Cove."

"The beach?"

"Yep."

"Not bad."

"A little slice of heaven," I said.

"Anybody with you?"

"You need confirmation?"

"If you have it."

"Routine?"

Meyer nodded.

"I don't know," I said. "Maybe I can see if anybody saw my car. I park it outside."

"All right," Meyer said. "When you can."

"Anything else?" I said.

"Yes. I'd like you to look at something."

He left and came back with a plastic evidence bag. He put it on the table.

"Have you seen this before?" he said.

"It's a Buck knife," I said.

"I asked if you've seen it before."

"This one? No. I have one like it, though."

"Where is it?"

I leaned back in the chair. "You're questioning me like a suspect now?"

"Am I?"

"You are. Don't they teach you any law around here?"

"No need to get upset, Mike."

"Plenty of reason. You hauled me down here on false pretenses. You put a knife in front of me. That the knife that cut Tatum Walker?"

"It was found at the scene."

"It's not my knife," I said.

"Where is your knife?"

"Am I a suspect or not?"

"Not," he said. "Yet."

"Then I'm free to leave," I said.

"Yes," Meyer said. "But it would go a long way if you could produce your knife."

"You want to see it? It's in the trunk of my car."

"That's great," Meyer said.

He walked me through the office and out a back door to the parking lot. I unlocked Spinoza's trunk and lifted the mat to recover my knife.

It wasn't there.

"Must be at my place," I said, trying to think of the last time I'd used it. "I'll find it for you."

"Let me help you out," he said. "It's back there in the interview room."

"I told you, that isn't my knife."

"And now you're under arrest."

"Oh, come on," I said.

"I need to advise you of your rights," Meyer said.

"This is absurd."

"You have the right to–"

"Yadda yadda. You can't possibly suspect me."

"—to remain silent—"

"I cut Walker's throat and left my knife there?"

"Anything you say can and will be used against you in a court of law. You have the right to an attorney—"

"Can it, Meyer. I am not waiving my rights. I want to call my lawyer."

"Sure," Meyer said. "But not on your phone. Empty your pockets, please."

I wanted to fight. I wanted to kick in a door. But Ira's voice was in my head, telling me to stay calm.

I gave up my car keys, wallet and phone.

"You know you can't search my phone without a warrant," I said.

"Back inside," Meyer said.

"Give me a phone."

"Come with me, Mike."

. . .

Meyer took me to the booking station. Fingerprints, mug shot. He didn't have to do it this way, but I'd shot my mouth off and he was pulling an authority move.

Then Meyer put me in an interview room with a desk and two chairs. There was a landline on the desk.

"You can make your call now," he said, and leaned against the wall.

"You staying?" I said.

"I won't interrupt you," Meyer said.

"Isn't a call to my lawyer confidential?"

"You can tell him where you are. You can talk things over confidentially when he gets here."

I picked up the phone and punched Ira's number.

"Hi, Ira."

"How's it going down there?"

"Oh, swimmingly." I looked at Meyer. "They've rolled out the red carpet, only with spikes on it."

"What?"

"They've got me under arrest for the attempt on Tatum."

"What!"

"Yeah. They actually think I did it."

Meyer made a motion with his finger for me to wrap it up.

"I'll be there in half an hour."

"Grand," I said. "We'll have ever so much fun. Tah!"

I hung up.

Meyer took me to a holding cell.

"We'll let you know as soon as he gets here," Meyer said. "You want some coffee?"

"You're offering me coffee?"

"We're not inhuman here," Meyer said.

"Can you throw in a couple of eggs over easy and hash browns?"

"How do you take your coffee?"

"Black, like my mood."

That brought a smile to his face.

I sat there looking at the faded green walls that had seen tens of thousands of hoods, killers, abusers, druggies, thieves, gangbangers, and more than a few innocents. Yet sometimes an innocent gets hosed. Was it my turn?

I did a hundred push-ups, some squats, and paced around. It was the waste of time that got me most. I'd eventually get out of this, but it was going to take precious hours, maybe days, and all the time Coby was out there somewhere.

Meyer came back with coffee in a Styrofoam cup and handed it to me through the bars.

Then left me alone.

The coffee tasted like rainwater squeezed out of a Seattle welcome mat.

Could that possibly be my knife? Could it have been stolen? By who?

And come on. Me slicing Tatum Walker? What was supposed to be my motive? Why did they suspect me in the first place? Did they have some lying witness? Anybody could have called them and set me up.

The whole thing was a setup.

But it would be my face on the newsfeeds.

And that's how Sophie would find out, unless Ira reached her first.

That'd be more cold, hard truth about being with Romeo. My life had been dedicated to truth, no matter how cold or hard. Truth was supposed to overcome all things.

Would it?

Forty minutes later, Meyer came back and escorted me to the interview room. Ira was there sitting at the table. I took the chair on the other side.

Meyer stayed standing. He placed a digital recorder on the table and pressed a button.

"This is Detective Eric Meyer from the LAPD Central Division. Today is Tuesday, March 20th, 11:31 a.m. We are here at the LAPD Central Division with suspect Michael Romeo and his lawyer, Mr. Ira Rosen. Present in the room are myself, Mr. Romeo, and Mr. Romeo's lawyer, Mr. Ira Rosen. We are about to conduct a recorded interview with Mr. Romeo. Mr. Romeo, could you please state your full name and confirm that you understand this conversation is being recorded?"

"Michael Romeo," I said. "I understand this farce is being recorded."

"Michael," Ira said.

"Good enough," Meyer said. "Mr. Romeo, I have given you your Miranda rights and you requested your lawyer to be present, is that correct?"

"You're darn tootin'," I said.

"And that will be the last time you address my client," Ira said. "You can talk to me."

"We have a knife that is a match for your client's knife," Meyer said.

"You know this how?" Ira said.

"He admitted as much," Meyer said.

"Before or after Miranda?"

Pause. "He was not in custody when I asked him."

"You made a mistake," Ira said.

"We'll let the DA hash that out."

"I don't deal in hash," Ira said. "Facts only. Now, I wish to speak to my client."

"Sure," Detective Meyer said. "You can have ten minutes."

Ira said, "And I don't have to remind you that you can't listen in or record anything."

"Of course," Meyer said. He stepped out of the room and closed the door.

"You had a conversation with this guy?" Ira said.

"I thought I was helping him out," I said. "Then he asks me where I was Monday night."

"And where were you?"

"Home. But nobody saw me."

"What's the deal with the knife?"

"The knife looks like mine. But it isn't mine. Or maybe it's mine and was stolen out of my trunk. Maybe it's at the Cove. I can't remember the last time I used it."

Ira rubbed his eyes. "So you're saying this is not just a misunderstanding, but a frame?"

"It looks that way," I said.

"What possible motive would you have for wanting Tatum Walker dead?"

"Maybe they'll ask ChatGPT for one."

"Don't joke about that," Ira said. "The robots will be ruling us soon enough. In the meantime, you're going to be arraigned. We'll see about bail. Depends on the charge."

"Fantastic," I said. "Ira, can you call Sophie and tell her what's going on?"

"Sure."

"We pledged our troth."

Pause. Ira said, "You asked her to marry you?"

"We mutually pledged," I said.

"Michael, I am stunned. In a good way, but stunned none-theless."

"How do you think I feel?"

"Good question," Ira said. "How do you feel?"

"Not too good, sitting here," I said. "I mean, what is she letting herself in for?"

"Not a dull life, that is for certain." He put his hand on mine. "I can attest to that, but you know what? I wouldn't have missed it for the world. God has a way of bringing people together who need each other."

"He works in mysterious ways, right?"

"But he works," Ira said. "That's the point."

W e talked for another ten minutes. Then there was a quick knock at the door and Meyer stepped in.

"We just conducted a search of your car, Mr. Romeo."

Ira said, "Wait, what? You can't do that."

"Incident to arrest," Meyer said.

"You know that a search incident has to be contemporaneous with the arrest, don't you?"

"Easy," Meyer said. "Maybe we can clear this up. May I ask your client a question?"

"You can ask," Ira said. "I'll advise him whether to answer."

"Fair enough. Mr. Romeo, what is your connection with something called The O'Hair Society?"

"None," I said.

"Ever heard of it?"

"That's two questions," Ira said. "I have one for you. What's your theory of this case?"

"I'm just going where the facts lead," Meyer said. "Doing my job."

"Well go ahead and do your job," Ira said, "and let me know how it goes. Right now, cut my client loose."

"One last item. Like I said, maybe we can clear this up."

"It's clear to me," Ira said. "You have the wrong man."

Meyer went to the door and motioned someone. The someone handed Meyer a tablet. Meyer closed the door and tapped the tablet.

"This is just preliminary," Meyer said. "We have a forensics intern here, so there'll be a more formal analysis later."

"Analysis of what?" Ira said.

Meyer put the tablet on the table. It was a split screen of two fingerprints. "On the left is the thumb print of your client. On the right is a thumb print taken from the knife in evidence. They're a match."

"Okay," I said. "Somebody stole my knife."

"Who might have done that?" Meyer said.

"The interrogation is over," Ira said. "I'll take him home with me now."

Meyer smiled. "You didn't really say that, did you?"

"It never hurts to ask," Ira said. "Michael, I will talk to you at the arraignment."

When Meyer put me back in the tank, I had a cellie. He was in dirty jeans and a short-sleeved shirt, his black hair was plastered down, and he had a couple of jailhouse neck tats. Could have been mid-twenties but the wrinkles at the corners of his eyes put ten years on him. He sat on the bench with his knees up, back against the wall.

When we were alone he said, "Hey."

I nodded, sat on the other bench.

"Sorry, man," he said. "Name's X."

"X?"

"Like the Elon Musk thing," he said. "I had it before. He stole it from me."

He laughed.

I didn't say anything.

"So what's your name, man?"

"Mike," I said.

"What they got you on?" he said.

"Listen, I'm a little tired," I said.

"That the way it's gonna be?" he said.

"To what way do you refer?"

He blinked. "Not sure what you just said."

"I'm sometimes not sure myself," I said.

"So what're you in for?"

I waved it off.

"Just passing the time," he said. "They think they got me on possession for sale."

"Yeah?"

"But they got it messed up," he said. "Get this. I go to this liquor store and I was gonna meet a guy, Ricky, a guy I met over in Simi on a job. I do handyman stuff, all kinds. I was fixing a garage door opener, and we started talking hustles, and he has this idea for one and asked would I be interested? And I say, I don't know, what's it about? He says meet me later at this liquor store. But he doesn't show, and I don't buy anything, I leave. Next thing you know the place is robbed, guy in a mask, and I look like the guy, his body I mean, and the owner describes me and the cops find me. And get this, I'm on parole, so they do a search and find the crank. Can you believe it?"

I shrugged.

"They messing you up, too?" he said. "Hey, you need somethin', maybe I can help."

"Why?"

"Gotta stick together," he said.

I gave him a long look. He seemed a little too anxious to get me to talk. I remembered something Ira taught me on a previous case.

"Maybe this is a Perkins," I said.

"A what?"

"Perkins."

"Who's that?"

I smiled. "You're a cop."

His face tried to hide it. For a split second, he didn't know what to do.

"Look, man–"

"No, you look," I said. "You're trying to get me to talk, it's obvious. You come off like a jailhouse lawyer, but you pretend not to know Perkins. That's Illinois v. Perkins, the Supreme Court, and every jailhouse lawyer knows it."

My cellie issued one word. It started with S.

"Cops can plant a guy in a cell to get a confession," I said. "But the court didn't address the situation where the suspect has previously invoked Miranda. Which is me. So you want my statement? I didn't do it. But you go on to have a fine career, officer."

He looked at me, shook his head. "I'm pretty impressed."

"You should be," I said. "I'm an impressive fellow."

He went to the bars and yelled. "Walking!"

A burly sheriff's deputy came over and let the guy out.

Me they put on a sheriff's bus with some other guys and drove us out to Castaic. It's a hot, unincorporated patch of ground north of Los Angeles. We passed by Six Flags Magic Mountain on the way, but didn't stop for a roller coaster ride or a churro. No fun.

The Pitchess Detention Center was a compound of four jail areas. The buildings looked like warehouses for airplane parts. It was surrounded by hot, parched, undeveloped ground where gila monsters and hearty jackrabbits played. It was as far removed from my beloved ocean as I could imagine, and I was imagining a lot.

Like would I ever get out of this? Or would jail-court-prison be my trajectory for the rest of my life?

Tatum Walker couldn't possibly believe I was the one who cut him. But that opinion wouldn't be admissible in a trial. The knife with my fingerprints would be, though.

And then there was Sophie. I wasn't about to let her become one of those women from the old Warner Bros. prison movies, who say, "I'll be waiting for you, Johnny."

They processed me in, gave me a set of blue jail togs. Then they took me and a group to watch an orientation video. Let's just say *Bringing Up Baby* it was not.

Next, they assigned me a bunk in one of the dorms. My dorm was mainly for misdemeanor convicts, parole violators waiting for a hearing, or guys like me whose next step is a preliminary hearing. The dorm held about ninety men on a series of two-tiered bunks. Just like summer camp. Or a sardine can.

On the bunk above mine sat a guy reading a graphic novel. He was in his late twenties, short and wiry. He looked at me as I tossed my county pillow on the bed.

"You my bunkie?" he said.

"I guess I am," I said.

"You a troublemaker?"

"Not in here."

"Good answer," he said. "Call me Pablo."

"Mike."

"What you in for?"

"Attempted murder," I said. "I didn't do it."

"Course not," Pablo said. "Nobody in here did it."

"I mean I really didn't do it."

"Sure, man. But I did."

"Yeah?"

"Beat a guy up good," he said. "He raped my sister."

"So you're doing time?"

"Four months to go till trial," he said. "My lawyer's trying to get me a better deal."

"Good luck," I said.

"What we all need, right?"

Just then a big guy with a bald head and broken nose walked by. Slowly, so I'd notice.

And he gave me the stink eye.

There's one in every joint. Picks out a guy, serves notice, marks his territory.

I looked away. I didn't want any trouble, just wanted to do my time, get out, get on with life. Let it be a nice, quiet stay for Mike Romeo.

Yeah, right.

I n the morning, an announcement came over the loudspeaker.

"We will be going to count in ten minutes. Get up, get dressed, and line up in the box."

The count box was a squared-off area where the barracks lined up.

Once more I got the stink eye from the guy with the broken nose. Was it just my natural charm?

I followed Pablo to the dining area and we sat at a table. Our delicious repast was Cheerios, two hard boiled eggs, two slices of bread, jelly, milk and OJ.

"Not enough for you," Pablo said.

"It's all right," I said. "I'm reducing."

"What?"

"Losing weight."

Pablo snorted. "You don't have no fat."

"What happens next?"

"We clean up. We get our linens, our new suits, boxers,

socks, towels. We go out to the count box again while they search the beds. Then they start the music."

"Music?"

"You know, the old music."

"Old?"

"Yeah, you know." Pablo made gestures like a conductor.

"Symphony music?" I said.

"Yeah, that's it. Supposed to be good for our brains, is what they say. After that, stuff you can do. There's yard time. We also got games."

"Games?"

"Dominoes, checkers, chess. You play chess?"

"A little," I said.

"Play you a game," Pablo said.

"Sure."

"I'm pretty good at it. Used to play a lot at MacArthur Park."

"I'll do my best," I said.

And I did. Pablo was good. He had the attitude of the street chess hustler, banging his pieces down and saying "Boom!" or "There we go!"

By move twenty or so I was a pawn ahead. Then someone joined us.

Stink Eye sat down, folded his hands on the table and said, "You look like somebody."

"Okay," I said.

"Who are you?"

"Mike." I extended my hand. He ignored it.

Pablo looked up from the board. "Hey man, we playing a game, huh?"

"Ain't talkin' to you," Stink said.

In rather colorful language, Pablo asked the intruder if he would like to have his, um, rear end kicked. I had to admire the moxie. Stink had maybe forty pounds on him.

Stink smiled. "We'll talk later, little guy." To me he said, "What you do on the outside?"

"I generally keep to myself," I said.

"Not here. You got to get along. I asked you a question."

Pablo started to say something. I put my hand on his arm.

I said, "Do you know what a cliché is?"

He looked momentarily flummoxed. "I didn't ask you that."

"I'm asking you," I said. "Because that's what you're in danger of becoming. The yard bull, the big fish, the cock of the walk, El Numero Uno, right? And you want to coax me into a fight. You want to mark your territory. That happens in every prison movie, which makes it a cliché, something that's been repeated so many—"

"Shut up!" Stink said.

"—times that it's boring. Like you are."

Pablo said, "Boom!"

Stink's jaw quivered. He stood. As he did, he swept his hand over the chess board, knocking off several pieces. Turned his back and walked on.

Pablo started to get up. I stopped him.

"Not now," I said.

"It's gonna have to happen," Pablo said.

"That's the cliché," I said. "Maybe I can rewrite it."

"Man, I don't get you."

"Sometimes, I don't even get myself," I said. "Pick up the pieces. I remember the position."

We didn't get to go on because my name was called for a bus ride back to court. For my arraignment. It's bad enough being bored in jail. But a prison bus ride is worse. No one sang camp songs.

Once inside the courthouse, I spent some time in a holding cell with six other sinners. Eventually, they brought us to a fenced-off jury box in the same courtroom Coby had been arraigned in.

Ira was already in court, using his braces to get around. He came over to talk to me.

"Still pressing attempted murder," he said. "Bail schedule calls for a million dollars."

"What's the good news?" I said.

"There is no good news," Ira said.

"Just thought I'd ask. How long is the farce going to go on?"

"It's well beyond farce. I'll move for a speedy trial, but you may be in for a few months."

"Get me some books," I said. "And talk to Sophie. Tell her what's going on and don't soft-pedal it."

"Sit tight."

"Is there any other way to sit in here?"

Ira went to a chair just inside the bar and sat next to another lawyer. They started to chat.

The guy sitting next to me was a wiry guy with greasy hair who smelled of mustard and old tires. He was chatting, too... to himself. His voice was a low mumble and every other word started with F or S.

I told him to knock it off.

He told me what I could do to myself, and went back to his mumbling.

I started to hum "My Mama Done Told Me."

A bailiff told us both to shut it.

When my case was called, Ira went through the routine. He entered a plea of not guilty, and asked that bail be based on assault with a deadly weapon, which was more

manageable. There was no witness and the evidence was likely
cooked.

The deputy DA, a woman named Marina Perez, who
looked as empathetic as Madame Defarge, pointed out the
heinous nature of the crime, the fingerprint evidence, and my
body size, "Which is a danger to most anyone."

She was right about that.

The judge took five seconds to set my bail at one million
dollars.

Back to jail I went.

At least I got lunch—a peanut butter and jelly sandwich,
apple, carrots, a couple of cookies and apple juice. Pablo
joined me.

"The guy's name is Sandoval," Pablo said.

"Who?"

"Your boyfriend."

"Okay."

"In for being an ex-felon with a gun."

"What's his sign?"

"It ain't funny, man. It's gonna happen."

"Let it," I said.

It happened out in the yard as I was soaking up some
vitamin D by the fence. Sandoval and three of his posse
gathered around.

"We got to get some things straight," he said.

"I've been thinking about that," I said.

"Oh, you been thinking? Whatta you been thinking?"

"I think we can settle this with a treaty," I said. "Let's say
you're Sparta and I'm Athens. We're in the middle of the Pelo-
ponnesian War."

He frowned.

"That's good for you," I said. "Sparta had the fighters.

Nobody wanted to mess with the Spartans. So you be Pleis-toanax, king of Sparta. Hear that? You're king. I'll be General Nicias of Athens. They worked out a treaty to avoid conflict for fifty years."

One of Sandoval's boys said, "Shut him up."

"Hear me out," I said. "Who wants trouble? I'll agree you're cock of the walk."

"You hear what he call you?" the boy said.

"Term of art," I said. "It means number one. You get to call yourself number one. In return, you agree not to start anything, and we all coexist in here doing our time."

"I'm gonna mess your face," Sandoval said.

"Now see?" I said. "That's not negotiating."

A small crowd was gathering. Pablo ran through it and up to Sandoval.

"Back off!" Pablo said.

Two of Sandoval's guys grabbed Pablo and pulled him away. Pablo kicked and cursed.

Sandoval smiled. And waited.

He wanted me to strike the first blow. That way he could shift the blame for any trouble to me, backed up by eyewitnesses.

I said, "How 'bout those Dodgers?"

He called me a few choice names.

"Let's play chess," I said.

That pushed his button. He came at me with an overhand right aimed at my head.

I bent back. The fist missed me. Sandoval was off-balance. I made my hand a flat blade and gave him a spear to the throat.

His face blanched. His eyes rolled up. His mouth made a sucking, scraping sound as he fought for breath.

And then Dante's Inferno broke loose.

Fists flew like confetti. Some landed on me. I spun, I elbowed, I landed blows to middles and heads.

A siren blared.

Then came the gas.

My eyes and throat caught fire. I doubled over and ran through bodies, the bodies scattering, the foul mess spilling over the entire yard. Guys were hacking, wheezing. Some tried to get in last licks.

I got out of the cloud and took a deep breath. It felt like I swallowed shards of glass. A taste like cayenne and dirty pennies assaulted my tongue. My eyes were fresh meat on a hot skillet.

I barked like a seal. I wasn't the only one. It was a mad circus, a scene out of Maxim Gorky.

I caught a glimpse of blue sky and stumbled forward.

Then got jumped from behind.

F lattened to the ground, a big body on top of me. Then hands on my face, iron finger pressing. The guy was trying to blind me.

Grappling training got me out. I gripped and flipped over, so I was on top.

It was Sandoval.

No negotiating now. There are times when you have to destroy. It's the fate of man and has ever been so. History is conquest. Kill or be killed.

I grabbed his hair and lifted, then pounded his face into the asphalt.

Again.

Again.

Kill. I didn't care.

A guard cared. Enough to whack my head with a baton. The Fourth of July exploded behind my eyes. I rolled off Sandoval and watched the fireworks display until it faded to black.

. . .

I came to with my head squeezing my brain and my eyelids scraping my eyeballs like sandpaper. Somebody was dabbing my head. I smelled blood.

"Just take it easy," the guy said.

Seemed a reasonable request. I was on a gurney. There was all sorts of coughing going on in the yard.

I didn't see Sandoval.

Then they moved me to the infirmary. I wasn't alone. I lay there and smelled the stink of human sweat batting up against industrial strength Lysol. A tired-looking doctor with wisps of gray hair gave me a once-over and gave me Imitrex, water, and an ice pack for the egg-shaped bump on the side of my head.

After about two hours sitting there thinking about life as dismal landscape a la Waiting for Godot, they took me back to my bunk.

Pablo was there.

"You the man," he said.

"Am I?"

"I told 'em," he said. "I told 'em it was all Sandoval. They figured it out. Look around. He ain't here."

"Is he dead?"

"Nah, man. Just looks like it. They took him out. He's going to North County."

That was the maximum-security facility at Pitchess complex.

"I just want to sleep," I said.

"Sleep like the man," Pablo said.

I closed my eyes and thought about the beach at Paradise Cove.

. . .

A guard woke me up. Said to come with him.

He took me to a room with a table and two chairs. In one of them was a guy in a suit and tie, a serious bureaucrat type. He nodded at me to sit. His ferret-like eyes scanned some papers in front of him.

"How's your head?" he said.

"Still attached," I said.

"My name's Adam Franklin," he said. "I'm with Sheriff's Admin. Wanted to talk to you about the incident."

"A mild word for it," I said.

"We're putting a report together," he said. "Can you tell me what happened?"

"Why don't you tell me?"

"I'd rather hear your take."

"I'd rather not," I said.

"You're in a position to help yourself."

"I don't do any talking unless my lawyer's with me."

"This isn't an interrogation," he said.

"I don't really care."

"You want to bring a lawyer in on this?"

"There's a reason you're asking, isn't there?"

He gave me a long weasel look. "It's my job."

"What you want to know is if I'm going to sue the department for almost killing me."

"That isn't what this is about."

"Of course it is. Let me put it to you this way. I like law, I like order, I like most cops and sheriff's deputies and prison guards. Sometimes one of them does something they shouldn't. Whoever whacked my bean is one of those. So, get him in a room, reprimand him and tell him not to do that anymore. How's that?"

Franklin tapped the table with his index finger.

"Interesting response," he said.

"I'm an interesting guy," I said.

"Would you be willing to sign a waiver of all claims?"

"Not to the claim that I'm an interesting guy."

He smiled. His teeth were yellow. "I'll have a waiver drawn up."

"You're a peach," I said.

After that, they took me to the infirmary again. The same doc shined a flashlight in my eyes, gave me a nystagmus test, had me stand on one foot and then the other, gave me Advil and told me not to watch too much TV, to rest as much as possible. The whole thing took less than ten minutes.

I used my phone time to call Ira. He'd seen online about the fight in the yard. I gave him the short version, up to my head smack.

He quoted Kipling at me. "If you can keep your head when all about you are losing theirs, and blaming it on you…"

"I've still got my head," I said.

"Then you're a man, my son," Ira said.

"Did you talk to Sophie?"

"I did."

"How'd she take it?"

"Let's just say she wasn't surprised," Ira said.

"Maybe now would be a good time for her to walk away."

"I can tell, after talking with her, that she is not that kind of woman."

"You can advise her," I said.

"I will not do that unless she asks me," Ira said.

"And if she does, what will you say?"

"I'll have to give that a good ponder," Ira said. "You are not the subject of easy answers. But I do have a word of advice for you."

"Bring it."

"Don't let her go."

.   .   .

S leep that night didn't come easy. My head was throbbing and Pablo was talking. He talked about wanting to open up a combination motorcycle repair shop and taco stand.

"Is that too crazy?" he asked.

"Everything else is crazy," I said. "So why not?"

"If you beat your rap, what're you gonna do?"

"I've always liked flowers," I said.

"Serious?"

"Sure."

He laughed. "It don't matter what you do, man. You got respect. Hey, maybe you could open a flower stand next to my shop."

"We can dream," I said.

"Call it Crazy Pablo's and Crazy Mike's."

"Fix a bike, eat a taco, smell the roses."

"Yeah!"

A fter breakfast I was told I had a visitor. I knew who it would be.

When I saw Sophie at the window, she was holding the handset to her ear as if it were a lifeline.

I sat, picked up my handset.

For a moment, we didn't say anything. Sophie studied my face.

"How bad is it?" she said.

"Just a little dinged up," I said.

"Right."

"Honest. A thunk on the head."

"Can Ira get you out of here?" she said.

"A bond would cost somebody a hundred grand," I said.

"I mean, they can't really believe you tried to kill Tatum Walker."

"They've got evidence."

"But what would be your motive?" she said.

"You're asking the right question," I said. "Ever thought about becoming a lawyer?"

"What's the answer?"

"I don't know," I said.

"This is so messed up," she said.

"As Hobbes said—"

"No philosophers," she said.

"I could have meant Calvin and Hobbes," I said.

"But you didn't. Mike, how can I help you?"

"You've got other things to do," I said.

"Answer the question," she said.

"Gosh, you're tough."

"Being with you does that to a person."

"There are other people you could be with," I said.

"Name one," she said.

I couldn't help smiling. She smiled, too.

Which made me want jump through the glass and hold her.

"I'll probably be in here awhile," I said.

"Then I'll just have to keep visiting you, won't I?"

"Just don't try smuggling in a cake with a file in it."

Sophie put her hand on the glass. I did the same, over hers.

She quoted Romeo and Juliet. "And palm to palm is holy palmers' kiss."

I quoted back. "Have not saints lips, and holy palmers too?"

"When you make bail," Sophie said, "you'll find out."

That was the highlight of my day. The routine wore on. Pablo and I played some chess. I went to the inmate library and checked out Dostoevsky's Crime and Punishment. It didn't look like anyone else had read it before.

Two days went by. Then I was told I had a call from my lawyer.

"Michael, you've made bail," he said.

"What? How?"

"I'm coming to get you out."

"Who?"

"That is confidential."

"Come on, Ira!"

"I must follow the code of professional ethics. See you in a couple of hours."

P ablo was sad to see me go.

"Don't forget me, man," he said.

"Not possible," I said.

"I hope you beat your thing."

"Same to you."

"I'm not kiddin' about my bike shop and your flower store."

"You got to have a dream," I said.

"Where can I find you?"

"Ira Rosen, Attorney at Law."

"Count on it," he said.

A round four I was processed out and in the van with my lawyer, confidante, and benefactor.

As we got on the freeway, I said, "You're not going to tell me who posted my bail?"

"The bondsman is Ernie Orsatti, but the donor wishes to be anonymous."

"It wasn't you, was it?"

"If it were, I wouldn't tell you."

"You'd make a great Sphinx," I said. "How is Tatum Walker?"

"He's still in the hospital."

"I want to see him," I said.

"That's not going to happen," Ira said. "Not yet. You're the defendant in his attempted murder."

"He can't believe I was the one."

"Why not?"

"He just… I want to tell him, face-to-face."

"I told you, you can't. Think about it for a moment."

"I'm tired of thinking," I said.

"What's the alternative?"

"Doing."

"Let's get you fed and rested," Ira said. "Then we'll talk about it."

"I'm tired of talking, too."

"I can see you're going to be pleasant company," Ira said.

"Who said anything about company? I'm going home."

"Stay with me, Michael."

"I need to see the ocean," I said.

Spinoza was at Ira's. He'd hired a neighborhood kid to drive it from the police impound lot. I grunted some words in parting, then drove back to the Cove.

As soon as I was on PCH, the smell of the Pacific lifted my spirits. When I got home, I changed and went down to the beach. I stood in the wet sand and took deep, restorative breaths.

Despite what I'd told Ira, I couldn't help thinking. I can't turn it off after all.

Who set me up? Who knifed Tatum Walker? How did my knife get stolen?

Where was Coby Keaton?

Why do Californians keep voting for agents of their own destruction?

Who paid for my bond?

As I headed back to my crib, I called Sophie.

"I'm home," I said.

"Yes!" Sophie said. "Ira told me you were getting out."

"Now if I can stay out," I said.

"Come over. I want to make you dinner."

"Rain check."

"Really?"

"I'm looking forward to microwaving a frozen burrito."

"Get over here," she said.

"I wouldn't be good company. I need some time to decompress."

"How much time?" she said.

"Not sure," I said.

"Don't make it too long, okay?"

"Okay."

"Will you put that in the form of a promise?"

"I don't know what's going to be happening," I said. "I only know I'm going to try to make things happen."

"What's that mean?" she said.

"You know me," I said.

"That's an ongoing project."

"No argument there," I said.

"Just see me soon, okay?"

"I promise," I said.

From my porch, I heard a familiar sound. "Hey, man!"

C Dog came bounding over to me like a happy spaniel looking for a tennis ball.

"You got sprung!" he said.

"Temporarily," I said.

"How come they think you did it?"

"A little thing called evidence," I said.

"No way! I'll testify for you. I'll tell 'em you didn't do it. I'll tell 'em you were with me."

"You can't lie under oath," I said. Even though people do it all the time.

I said, "How's the finger?"

"Really hurts," he said. He held up his hand and tried to flex it.

"Give it time," I said.

"Life really sucks, doesn't it?"

"It tries to," I said. I almost left it there, but I feel a responsibility to C, having spent time teaching him the art of overcoming. I have to ride that train to the end.

"The only question," I said, "is how are you going to respond?"

"We could have a beer," he said.

"You finish your antibiotics?"

"Almost."

"No beer," I said. "Want a Coke?"

And that's what we drank, sitting on the porch and listening to the waves. It was good to talk, to get back the feel of being at home.

But I've learned not to lean on that feeling.

That night I dreamed about Tatum Walker. I dreamed I saw him on the street, called out to him, and he just turned his back and walked away.

Which is why I knew I had to see him.

I t was ten the next morning when I got to the hospital. At the front desk, I said I was there to visit Tatum Walker. After tapping a few keys, the formidable woman behind the glass said, "He is not having visitors, except for family."

"How about his lawyer?" I said.

"Are you his lawyer?"

I slipped Ira's card through the window opening.

"You're Ira Rosen?" she said.

"I work for him," I said. "This is a professional call."

She looked at her monitor. "You'll have to check in on the fourth floor for further instructions."

"I can do that," I said.

She printed out a sticker that said VISITOR and gave it to me. I slapped it on my shirt.

The fourth floor had the usual hospital activity. Nurses, staff, walking from place to place, all business. If you keep your head down you can sometimes walk around yourself, without getting called out.

Except when there's a cop standing by one of the doors.

A policewoman to be exact. Young, smallish, bored.

I walked up to her, smiled and nodded. You do that and usually get a like response from a civil servant. She only nodded.

"I'm here to see Tatum Walker," I said.

"Only family," she said. "Who are…" Her eyes widened. She recognized me.

Taking a step back, she put her hand on her sidearm.

"On your knees," she said. "Hands on your head."

"Stop it, will you?" I said.

"On your knees!"

"I'm out on bail," I said. "And you're not about to shoot me. Come on, follow me."

I pushed open the door and went in.

"Stop!" she said.

But I was inside.

Tatum Walker was propped up in bed, a bandage around his throat, reading a book.

The policewoman followed.

"Sir, you must leave right now!"

Tatum Walker waved his arms, shook his head. He motioned for the cop to come to him.

Looking extremely pained, she went to the bed. Walker had her lean over. I heard the low rasp of his voice saying something.

When the policewoman straightened up, she looked at me. "He says you didn't do it."

"He's right," I said.

"I still can't let you…"

"You're doing fine," I said. "It's a lot to take in at once. Call your superiors, tell them I'm here and have them contact the DA's office. See if we can't set up a meeting."

She hesitated, then looked at Tatum. He nodded approval. That didn't clear up her consternation, but it did get her to take out her phone. She stepped outside the room.

Tatum put out his hand. I took it.

In a painfully low whisper, he said, "I know it wasn't you, brother."

"Any idea who it was?"

He shook his head.

I squeezed his hand, released it.

That's when the doctor stormed in.

His badge said Dr. Pangaj Agerwal. "You cannot be in here," he said.

"I'm friend, not foe," I said.

"Is he talking? Are you talking, Tatum?"

Tatum smiled.

"That's it," Dr. Agerwal said. "Please leave the room."

"We're waiting for the DA to show up," I said.

"Wait outside then, please."

Tatum gave me a thumbs-up.

Outside, the policewoman was finishing up her call.

When she parked her phone, I said, "Any luck?"

"I was told to keep you here," she said. Her nameplate said Alonzo.

"I won't be any trouble, Officer Alonzo," I said. "And I'll tell 'em I busted in the room before you could stop me, and that you acted properly and with composure."

"I wasn't exactly composed," she said.

"Under trying circumstances, you were. Can I get you a coffee?"

"This is a little… weird."

"How long you been on the force?"

"Three years."

"And they gave you this duty?"

"We were shorthanded."

"You stepped up."

She didn't look convinced.

"The greatest obstacle to being a hero is the fear of being thought a fool," I said. "True heroism is to resist the doubt. Do you take anything in your coffee?"

An hour later we were joined by another uniformed cop, Detective Meyer and a Deputy DA named Randall Lake.

I greeted them with courtesy and restraint. They treated me like Sasquatch in running shoes. Meaning the cops were not going to let me leave. Calmly, I told them why I was there, extolled the stellar performance of Officer Alonzo, and advised them to go in and hear what Tatum Walker had to say.

With a frustrated huff, Meyer went in, followed by Lake.

That left me outside with two uniformed police officers. Officer Alonzo and a male officer named Shadwell.

"You know what I used to like about LAPD?" I said.

Alonzo said, "What?"

"Did you ever watch *Adam-12*?"

Alonzo shook her head.

"I've seen it," Shadwell said. "Kent McCord spoke at the Academy when I was there."

"I watched it as a kid in New Haven, with my dad," I said. "Local channel ran it. It takes place in the 1970s. I always liked the hats. You guys don't wear hats anymore."

"Sometimes," Shadwell said. "Parade day, dress day."

"But out in the field," I said. "It gave you a look of author- ity. You guys don't get the respect you deserve anymore."

"We really shouldn't be talking to you," Alonzo said.

"Is there no civility left in this world?" I said "No conviviality?"

The two officers said nothing.

"I guess not," I said. "Just remember, since I'm not in custody, any spontaneous statement I make may be used against me in court. So here comes my statement. I am inno- cent. I am as innocent as Dreyfus."

"The actor?" Alonzo said.

"The French army officer."

Neither of them looked like they knew what I was talking about. I was going to ask if they'd heard of Emile Zola, who got Dreyfus out of Devil's Island, but Meyer and Lake came back out.

"New information has come to our attention," Lake said.

"Do tell," I said.

"I think you know."

"I'd just like to hear it from you."

"You can hear it from your lawyer," Lake said. "Tell Mr. Rosen I'll call to set up a meeting."

"Exonerated," I said.

"You're not off the hook yet," Meyer said.

"There's still a hook?"

Meyer said, "I ask that you leave the premises. Officer Alonzo will escort you out."

"With pleasure," I said. "I love our men and women in blue."

Officer Alonzo smiled.

I called Ira from the parking structure.

"A new day dawns," I said.

"What's happening?" Ira said.

"I just left Tatum Walker, Detective Meyer, and a deputy DA. Walker told them I wasn't the guy."

"Wait . . . what?"

"I'm leaving the hospital now," I said. "The DA's going to call you. But as of this moment, I'm free as the Bluebird of Paradise."

There was a long pause.

"Ira?"

"There are times when you surprise even me," Ira said.

"That is my calling, and my pleasure."

"Come over and let's talk."

"Not yet."

"What are you going to do now?"

"Look for more surprises."

I drove to Sonhouse. I didn't want to announce myself, so I waited till somebody came out the front door. I caught it before it closed and went in.

In the common room, there were some men two playing chess—I knew them, same guys—some watching *Gilligan's Island* on TV.

And on the far side, I saw Nathan White talking to two

guys sitting at a table who looked like they didn't want to be talked to.

They didn't see me until I was almost on them.

Nathan White turned white. "Whoa, whoa, wait!"

"It's okay, Nathan."

"You can't be here!"

"It's not what you think," I said. "I just saw Tatum."

"What?"

"In the hospital. He can talk. Barely. He said I didn't do it."

"Whoa, wait…"

"He told that to the cops and the DA."

"You leave him be," one of the guys said. He was tall and gaunt, like an undertaker out of Dickens.

"It's all right, Sam," Nathan White said.

"Not all right," Sam said. "This's our house."

The other guy, short and nervous, with a tic that jerked his head to the side every few seconds, said, "Everything's falling from the sky, Gog and Magog, moon turning to blood."

"Is there somewhere we can talk?" I said to Nathan White.

"Blood and fire," Nervous Tic said.

"Come on," White said. He walked away from the table, went across the room. I followed. He stopped near the kitchen pass-through window.

"What is this about the police and DA?" he said.

"Your boss gave them a statement. He knows I didn't do it."

"Then who did?"

"He doesn't know. He just knows it wasn't me."

Nathan White rubbed his face. "We're all a little shaky right now," he said.

"Sure."

"The police have already been here. That makes a bunch of the guys nervous."

"Your boss almost got killed," I said. "The police have to do their job."

"Should you be here?"

"My own life is on the line," I said.

"I'm sorry for that. How can I help?"

We went to a side door marked Emergency Exit Only. Nathan pushed it open. Outside was a passageway between Sonhouse and the adjoining building. It was empty except for some garbage scattered around. It opened up onto the street on both ends.

Pointing, Nathan said, "He was found right over there."

"Who found him?"

"A woman who came into the passageway to sleep."

"What was Tatum doing out here?"

"He likes to take a look before closing things down for the night."

"That's his regular practice?"

"If there's somebody needing shelter, he likes to be on hand to help them inside."

"Thanks," I said. "I'll just have a look around."

"I'll be inside if you need me," Nathan said.

I didn't expect to find anything after a police scrub. I tried to visualize how it might have happened. How did somebody get at Tatum Walker from behind? Had the person been lying in wait? There wasn't anything to hide behind. No dumpster. No boxes.

What if there were two perps involved? What if one of them was posing as a distressed homeless guy? That'd give distraction for the cutter to move in.

I made my way to the access point of the alley on San Julian Street. And remembered there was a reading room of the

O'Hair Society around somewhere. I looked it up on my phone. It was on Ninth. I took a walk.

The city was doing some work on Broadway, leaving a mess for the masses to deal with. It's also called urban renewal or quality-of-life upgrade or your tax dollars at work. But it didn't look like much work was going on at the moment. Your tax dollars at leisure.

At Seventh there was gridlock in the intersection featuring a city bus, honking cars, and at least two upraised fingers. The music of the brotherhood of man.

My phone buzzed. It was Ira. I ignored it.

Years ago, there were Christian Science Reading Rooms all over the place, evangelizing for the doctrines of Mary Baker Eddy. The O'Hair Society version was in that grand tradition, with a nod toward "the most hated woman in America" as Madalyn Murray O'Hair was once dubbed. She apparently wore that as a badge of honor.

Inside was a teacher's desk with a magenta-haired person of not immediately discernible gender. Heavy eye makeup, studs in nose and ears, black sweatshirt over body without protrusions. He, she, or other was reading a book, looked up and did not smile.

"Help you?" The voice was a muffled toot.

"I wanted to do some reading," I said.

Toot put the open book face down on the table. It was Existentialism & Humanism by Jean-Paul Sartre.

"What kind of reading?"

"I don't know," I said. "What would you recommend?"

"What are you looking for?"

"Answers, I guess."

"You know about The O'Hair Society?"

"Not really."

"Maybe I can help." Toot stood. Was about 5'5". "What's your name?"

"Phil," I said.

Toot extended a hand. I took it and gave it the dead fish. Toot's hand squeezed, but only enough to compress a sponge.

"I'm Glenna. We're about free thought here."

"That sounds good," I said.

"It is. You have any strong religious or philosophical beliefs?"

I shook my head. "I guess I'm searching."

"We like that," Glenna said. "The main thing is to think for yourself. Let's start with religion. Would you consider yourself a religious person?"

"Not really," I said. "I mean, I guess there's a God."

"That might be a bad guess. Were you raised in a religion?"

"We didn't go to church," I said.

"Did you go to college?"

"Nah. After high school I worked at KFC, then became a mechanic."

"What brought you in here?"

"Well, you know, the world is kind of crazy right now, and I just want to find something solid."

"You got that right. But it's not religion. That always ends up in war. Look, why don't you browse our bookshelf and see if anything looks interesting to you. It's arranged alphabetically by author. You're welcome to read anything you like."

"Thanks a lot."

"And here." Glenna reached for a pamphlet from a stack on the desk. "You can have this."

It was a stapled booklet with a plain blue cover. *Introduction to Atheism* by Weston Elliott.

I put the pamphlet in my back pocket and went to the bookshelf. It was filled with paperbacks, well used, and a few hardbacks. At the head of the shelf was Rules for Radicals by Saul Alinsky. I knew the title, of course, as it was big in the 60s. I'd never read it. Now seemed like a good time.

My phone buzzed again. I didn't answer.

I went to a soft chair by the window and opened Alinsky. And found this in the introduction:

Lest we forget at least an over-the-shoulder acknowledgment to the very first radical: from all our legends, mythology, and history (and who is to know where mythology leaves off and history begins—or which is which), the first radical known to man who rebelled against the establishment and did it so effectively that he at least won his own kingdom—Lucifer.

Funny and not funny how Lucifer kept showing up. I leafed through it and found an amalgam of pious phrases and strategies aimed at shaking things up and tearing things down. I tossed it on a table.

Then I looked at Elliott's pamphlet. It was written in college freshman style: a Q and A form, nothing new from a philosophical standpoint. Because there is nothing new, just reworking what skeptics of the past had written before. I recognized some warmed over Bertrand Russell, a big dollop of Robert Ingersoll, a lot of Sam Harris. I pretended to be interested.

Glenna was watching me over the Sarte book.

I held up the pamphlet. "Hey, this is pretty interesting. Does Mr. Elliott ever come in here?"

"Sure," Glenna said with a happy trill. "If you wait around, you could maybe meet him."

I did wait around. Ira called again. I texted him—*Busy. Don't wait up.*

A little after one, while I was flipping through a book by four "eminent" atheists giving their best shots and missing the targets, Weston Elliott walked in.

I recognized him from pictures. He was a lean six feet or so, wearing tan slacks and black loafers and a light-blue, business-casual shirt. His hair was black and slicked down. He approached the desk.

Behind him was a guy more my size, dressed in a gray linen suit with a white shirt and open collar. He wore shades. I pretended to be interested in the book.

Glenna said something to Elliott. A moment later he and his goon came over.

"I'm surprised to see you here," Elliott said.

I looked up. "Do we know each other?"

"I know who you are," Elliott said. "Why aren't you in jail?"

"You haven't heard?" I said. "I didn't do it. I thought maybe you might know who did."

The bodyguard expanded his chest, like a blowfish on the defensive.

Elliott remained cool. "Why would I? I don't like Tatum Walker, but I don't wish him dead. I prefer a verbal battlefield."

"Me, too."

He gave me a half smile. "Maybe sometime we can have a chat. But right now I have business to attend to."

"Go right ahead," I said.

"I'm going to ask you to leave."

"Thanks for asking," I said. "I may stay and do some more reading."

"Then I'm telling you to leave," Elliott said. Bodyguard took a step toward my chair.

I stood.

"Isn't this a public place?" I said.

"It's my place," Elliott said. "As the old sign says, we reserve the right to refuse service to anyone."

"Let's go," Bodyguard said.

I sized him up. It would be a tussle. But I had one of my

nicer Tommy Bahama shirts on and didn't feel like getting it ripped.

With a nod, I sauntered to the door. Bodyguard followed.

Outside, I stopped.

"Move along," Bodyguard said.

I didn't.

"That the way it's gonna be?" he said.

"Do you have authority over the public sidewalk?" I said.

"You wanna see?"

"Relax," I said. "I'm just deciding which way to go."

"Get lost," he said. His phone buzzed in his pocket. He took it out and turned his back to me.

On impulse, I took my phone out and held it over his shoulder and took a pic.

He whipped around. "What're you doing?"

"See ya," I said. But I only got two steps before his big paw grabbed my shoulder and yanked me back.

"Whudjoo just do?" he said.

As I pocketed my phone, I knocked his arm away. He put his own phone away and grabbed a fistful of my Tommy Bahama.

I reached up and put a vice grip on his throat. His eyes bulged. He let go of my shirt and put both hands around my wrist. That left his belly open. I gave him a left to the liver. He *oomphed*, but a fighter's instinct brought his own left toward my jaw.

I pulled back. He missed.

Now his head was vulnerable. I normally don't like to punch the face. It can easily break little bones in your fist. But if you aim the knuckles just right and get him in the jaw hinge, you can mess up his chewing ability for a long time.

Which is what I did. He'd be sucking Ensure for weeks.

I walked backward a few steps. He was stomping around in pain.

I didn't wait for his recovery. I got gone.

Αnd hoofed it back to Sonhouse to get my car. When I
got to it, somebody was waiting for me.

It was the nervous tic guy. His eyes were wild. He had a
fork in one hand, and a table knife in the other.

He held up the knife, then put the fork across it forming a
cross. He thrust the cross toward my face.

"Resist the devil," he said. "And he will flee!"

"Excuse me?" I said.

He shook the "cross" at me. "Flee!"

"Hold on there, sport."

Nervous Tic made a slicing motion across his neck.

That got my attention. "Talk to me."

"You are the father of lies."

"All right, listen. You think I'm the devil or something?"

He nodded.

"Do I look like the devil?" I said.

"He can appear like an angel," Tic said.

"Okay. Do I look like an angel?"

He frowned. I embellished the point. "If I wanted to look
like an angel, you think I'd be wearing a Hawaiian shirt and
jeans? I'd have a white robe, wouldn't I?"

He lowered his cutlery. "I don't know," he said.

"I work for a lawyer."

The cross came back up. "Lawyers are of the devil!"

"Sometimes," I said. "I'll grant you that. But this lawyer is
a rabbi, a believer in Jehovah."

"He is?"

"And a good man," I said. "Did you see Tatum Walker get
cut?"

Nod.

"Can you describe who did it?" I said.

He shook his head.

"Anything at all about him?"

Another shake.

"Why didn't you come forward?" I said.

"The devil," he said.

"Forget the devil!"

That spooked him. He made the cross again. Then he threw the silverware at me and ran.

Oh, he would make a fine witness. I couldn't wait to tell Ira about him.

W hen I walked into Ira's, he was at his desk tapping away.

Without looking away from his monitor, he said, "I shudder to ask."

"Mind if I make a sandwich?" I said, going straight to the kitchen.

"You have some explaining to do," Ira said.

"You sound like Ricky Ricardo," I said.

"Don't deflect."

In the refrigerator I found some Hebrew National corned beef, sauerkraut, and rye bread. I made a quick sammy, added some deli mustard, wrapped a paper towel around it and joined Ira by plopping in the reading chair by the window. I took a healthy bite.

"Why did you go silent on me?" Ira said.

I put my finger up to finish my chew, then said, "I thought you needed some peace and quiet."

"Michael, please."

I gave him the rundown right up to the convo with Nervous Tic. When I finished, Ira was holding the bridge of his nose and looking down.

My sandwich was almost gone.

"Just another day at the office," I said.

"You think this fellow really saw the attack?" Ira said.

"Does it matter? He can't describe the attacker. And what a witness he'd be. He'd probably accuse the judge of being the devil."

"There have been times I wanted to do the same," Ira said. "Let's have a look at the picture you took of the guy's phone. Send it to me."

When he got it, he put it on his monitor. "It looks like EZ2 maybe 8 or 3, hard to see the rest."

"Can you make out any of the messages?"

"A word or two maybe. I'll run it through a program."

"Nail this guy," I said.

"For what?" Ira said.

"For Tatum."

"We don't have enough evidence to presume that," Ira said. "Or have you forgotten the Golden Thread woven through Anglo-Saxon law?"

"Court recesses for lunch?"

"The presumption of innocence."

I sighed. "What if I went away for a while?"

"Away?"

"Far away. Maybe herd sheep. Grow tomatoes. Take a vow of silence."

"You? Silent?"

I did the mime thing with my hands against invisible glass.

"It won't work," Ira said. "You belong here."

"Nobody belongs here anymore," I said.

"You have duties, then. And you're still not off the hook. We have a meeting with the DA tomorrow."

"Oh, goodie."

"Why don't you go outside and read?"

I stood. "I'll take a drive instead."

"Where?"

"To look for some sheep."

I got in Spinoza and drove. I took surface streets into Hollywood, letting the jumble in my mind try to find some coherence. It didn't.

So I kept driving, taking Cahuenga into the Valley. At least now I knew where I was going.

I pulled to a stop on Sophie's street, a block away from her building. She'd be home in an hour or so. That would give me plenty of time to decide if I should see her or not. I'd have to sometime. Wasn't it Twain who said never do today what you can put off till tomorrow?

As I was contemplating, a gray Ford drove past me and parked at the curb directly across from Sophie's.

A guy got out. He leaned against the hood of his car, arms folded, and looked up toward Sophie's window. Was this that creep she'd reported to me? He fit her description.

I got out and walked up the sidewalk. The guy gave me a cursory look, then went back to watching the building. I walked past his car, then came around to him.

"What're you doing?" I said.

He dropped his arms. "What?"

"I asked what you're doing."

"Mind your own business," he said.

"You're going to tell me what you're doing, or get a broken bone or two."

"Hey man, come on."

"I'm not going to ask you again."

"Did she hire you?" he said. "You following me?"

"Why don't you tell me who hired you."

"Leave me alone."

I took his arm and twisted it behind him, turned him, and pressed him down on the hood.

"Talk," I said.

He shrieked. "Who are you?"

"A concerned citizen."

"It hurts!"

"Then talk."

"Okay, okay! Let me up!"

Feeling more charitable than I thought possible, I released him.

He stood up. There were tears in his eyes. He rubbed his shoulder.

"What're you gonna do to me?" he said.

"I don't know yet," I said.

"You don't know the whole story."

"Tell it to me."

"She won't let me see my kids," he said. "She's supposed to let me see my kids."

"Who?"

"Who do you think?"

"Tell me."

"My ex, that's who."

"Your ex?"

"My ex-wife, yeah, as if you didn't know. You gonna beat me up now? Is that why she hired you?"

The guy wasn't acting.

"Fill me in," I said. "Maybe I made a mistake."

"Mistake! You almost took my arm off!"

"It still works," I said.

"I just want to see my kids."

"Why can't you?"

He didn't answer.

I said, "Is there a court order?"

He nodded.

"I'm guessing not in your favor," I said.

"She lied through her teeth! And the judge bought it."

"This isn't the way to handle it," I said.

"What do you know?"

"The law."

"You a lawyer?"

"I work for one."

"So what should I do?"

"I'm not a judge," I said. "I don't know you or the facts or how you look under oath. But I'll tell you from experience it's better to follow the law than take it into your own hands. Don't do anything stupid. Like stay here."

He shook his head in the giving-up way. Then he got in his car and drove off.

I thought about doing the same thing. But when I got back in Spinoza, I saw Sophie's car pulling into the driveway.

I gave her ten minutes. I took the stairs to the second floor, knocked on her door, and put my face right up to the peep hole.

"Mike!" She opened the door. "You're here!"

"Yes," I said. "What were your other two wishes?"

She wrapped her arms around me, then pulled me into the best kiss this side of The Princess Bride.

We went into the living room. Sophie said she'd like a glass of wine and would I? I said yes. She went to the kitchenette and came back with two glasses of red. We sat like civilized people. One of us, anyway.

"I encountered that guy who was looking at your window," I said.

"What?"

"He was out there when I got here," I said. "Turns out he wasn't looking for you."

"Who then?"

"Is there a woman on this floor, about your age, with a couple of kids?"

"Yes, two doors down. She keeps to herself, pretty much."

"It's the guy's ex-wife. They're fighting over the kids."

"Ah," Sophie said. "So he's trying to intimidate her."

"I told him to knock it off," I said. "To keep things legal."

"Good advice."

"Not advice I always follow myself," I said, and took a sip of wine.

She didn't answer at first, then said, "You have something you want to tell me?"

"Don't I always?"

"I'm listening."

"You know, you're a teacher, a pedagogue, a guider of young minds. When you come home at night and sit with a friend and talk about your day, it's about the challenges and the victories—especially the victories—when something clicks in a student, they get it, and you feel the reward of that, a satisfaction unlike anything else."

"That's true," she said.

"But when I talk about my day, it usually involves how much damage I did."

"I'll bite," she said. "How much?"

"I had a fight with a guy on the street. On the plus side, I saw Tatum Walker. He told the police I didn't do it."

"That's fantastic!"

"And that was my day," I said.

Holding her wine glass in both hands, Sophie gave me a long look. "Well, there's one metaphor I'm not going to use to describe your life."

"What's that?" I said.

"A box of chocolates."

"How about a cache of explosives?"

"You never know which one's going to go boom," she said.

"Nailed it."

"How about a pizza?" she said.

"I don't get that metaphor," I said.

"No, Mr. Genius. I mean let's order a pizza."

We had one delivered. A Hawaiian style. We munched and talked about Jane Austen. Sophie loved Jane Austen, her timeless style, the fact that her name didn't originally appear in the books, how she died too soon. And how she wrote so insightfully about love yet never married, dying too soon at the age of forty-one.

Then she said, "Have you considered that whoever is setting you up, and whoever tried to kill Tatum Walker, may be a person or persons who have made an actual deal with the devil?"

"You believe that can happen?"

"You've read Faust."

"That's fiction."

"Whether or not there's an actual devil, if someone believes it is so and makes an explicit plea for his power, that will have an effect on their brain and their actions."

"Sophie Montag, you're a philosopher."

"I have to keep up with you, Romeo."

"I think they call that having a tiger by the tail."

"Or a bull by the horns," she said. "And that's enough metaphoring for one night.

She lifted her glass. I lifted mine and she clinked it.

"We make a good team," she said.

"I'll drink to that," I said.

.   .   .

I t was cold when I got back to the Cove. C Dog was sitting on my porch, a guitar in his hands

"Look!" he said, and plunked a couple of chords.

"How's it feeling?" I said, sitting next to him.

"It freakin' hurts. But I'm playing!"

"Just like life," I said.

"Huh?"

"You've got to play through the pain," I said.

He blinked a couple of times. "I don't like pain."

"It's how you deal with it that counts."

"How do you deal with it?"

"I think about it, then make a move. Sometimes you fight, sometimes you retreat. The trick is knowing which move is best."

"Do you always know?"

"Nope," I said.

C Dog plunked another chord. "I'm glad you're not in jail," he said.

"Stone walls do not a prison make, nor iron bars a cage."

"Man, the stuff you come up with."

"That's from a poet," I said. "Richard Lovelace."

"Did he do time?"

"He did," I said. "A couple of times. During the English Civil War in the 1600s. But out of that he produced some great verse. What does that tell you?"

He pondered. Shook his head.

"No pain, no gain," I said.

"Wow." He played a chord. "Ow."

"You're gaining," I said.

T he next day, Ira and I went to the DA's office in the refurbished Hall of Justice downtown.

In a conference room we met with Deputy DA Randall Lake and Detective Eric Meyer. Neither of them looked pleased.

"Understand," Lake said, "that we can proceed with the case even with Mr. Walker's hesitation."

"You mean denial," Ira said.

"There is still evidence," Lake said. "The knife."

"But no motive," Ira said.

"That usually comes last."

"What about other suspects?" Ira said.

"Like Weston Elliott," I said.

"Our investigation is ongoing," Meyer said. "And that still includes you."

"Come on, will you?" I said.

"Michael," Ira said.

"No," I said. "You know I didn't do it."

"We are considering withdrawing the complaint," Lake said, though it took effort.

"That's a start," Ira said.

"But we don't want you leaving town, as they say," said Meyer.

"This town ain't big enough for you and me, Sheriff," I said.

"Michael!" Ira said.

"I'm not going anywhere," I said. "We still have a client out there I'm looking for."

"As long as you don't muck around in our investigation," Meyer said.

"Define mucking," I said.

"You know what I mean," Meyer said.

"I'll make sure he does," Ira said.

. . .

D riving back to Ira's in his van, Ira said, "You do understand mucking, right?"

"I don't muck," I said. "I discover."

"You also break china."

"You're not very confidence building," I said.

"Confidence is not what you need," Ira said.

"What do I need?"

"Restraint."

"Restraint is for dead people," I said.

"Unrestraint makes people dead," Ira said.

"Some people deserve to die."

"And you're the one to decide?" Ira said.

"Sometimes the decision is forced," I said.

"Let the law decide."

"Sometimes the law is late."

"I shall tell you a story. It seems a wise and just king possessed a precious ring. It had the power to make the wearer beloved by both God and man. The king had three sons living in different cities. He couldn't give each of them the ring, so he had a goldsmith create two rings identical to the real one. Each son got a ring when the king died."

"That's touching," I said.

"I'm not finished. The sons found out what their father had done, and got into a fight about who had the real ring. They took it to a judge, a wise judge. After he heard the arguments, he advised the sons live as if each had the real ring, embodying its power to be beloved by God and man. In this way, they would each honor their father's memory and the essence of the ring. Do you see?"

"All that glitters is not gold?"

"No, you oaf. You can choose to follow the spirit of the law, not just the technicalities, and thus live a just and virtuous life. Not everything is settled with a fight."

"But some things are," I said.

"And how do you find out which things are, without undue harm?"

"Do unto them before they do unto you?"

"Restraint," Ira said.

"When do we eat?" I said.

"I'm so glad these little talks make such an impression on you."

A t Ira's we did eat, a kosher hot dog for me. Soup for Ira. Then Ira sat at his computer with me next to him.

He said, "I did a general search for EZ2812 and I got a flight tracker for EasyJet, a British airline. Flight 2812 was a flight from Corfu, Greece to Bristol. I doubt this is our messenger."

"I must agree," I said.

"But perhaps EZ could be short for Easy. Now, what is easy about the number 2812? It could be anything. It could be a birthday, December 28, with the numbers transposed. It could be the last four digits of a phone number. It could be a street address."

"Easy Street," I said.

"Now you're thinking."

"Can you do anything intelligence-wise?"

"Everything I do is intelligence-wise."

"You know what I mean," I said. "Find out where this name is registered, and thereby find the phone?"

"That may be impossible," Ira said.

"So it will take you a little longer than usual," I said.

"Thanks for the confidence."

"Don't restrain yourself," I said.

. . .

I went out back and called Coltrane Smith. Left a message. I sat on the bench under the magnolia tree. A couple of doves sat on a phone wire running along the fence line. They seemed perfectly content. They say doves get married. Or, if you will, mate for life. I wondered if that was Mr. and Mrs. Dove up there, maybe house hunting for a new nest.

Maybe it was a sign. Mr. and Mrs. Dove. Me and Sophie. Birds on a wire, all of us.

And just like that, the doves shot away. A big, black crow swooped down and chased them, cawing like a demon.

Great. Maybe that was a sign, too.

I didn't have time to figure it out because a familiar voice shouted, "Young man!"

Mrs. Morgenstern was looking at me over the fence. She had to be standing on something. She wore a sun bonnet and held a trowel.

I went over.

She said, "I wonder if you might help me."

"What can I do for you, Mrs. Morgenstern?"

"I can't open a bottle. Do you think you could do that for me?"

"Not only think," I said. "I can guarantee it."

"Come around to the house." She stepped down and her head disappeared behind the fence.

So ordered, I went out the side gate and over to Mrs. Morgenstern's home. I waited at the front door until she opened it. She motioned into the living room. The house smelled like a two-day old egg-and-onion sandwich.

"You just wait here," she said, motioning to the sofa. She toddled off.

The TV was on. A religious program. A preacher—wearing jeans, a sweatshirt and white running shoes—stood on a stage and behind a podium. "The storms of life will come, you can't stop them," he said. "And they'll test what you've built. And there will be a test at the judgment seat of Christ."

"Here it is," Mrs. Morgenstern said, handing me a bottle of Bragg Apple Cider Vinegar.

"I need it for my bloating," she said. "And what comes along with that." She put her hand to her mouth and whispered, "Gas."

The words *over sharing* came to mind, but I merely nodded. I twisted the cap off, then gave it a half twist back on and handed it to her.

"You're going to make some woman very happy one day," Mrs. Morgenstern said. "So hop to it."

The preacher said, "He is like a man building a house, who dug down deep and laid the foundation on rock."

"Did you hear what I said?" Mrs. Morgenstern said.

Hardly. I was looking at the TV screen. The preacher's words were on the bottom of the screen, followed by *Lk. 6:48.*

A Bible verse.

Pow.

"Enjoy your vinegar," I said, moving quickly toward the front door.

"Wait a minute! I want to talk—"

"Another time," I said. "I promise."

And I was out the door.

I ra looked up as I charged in.

"What's going on?" he said.

"EZ," I said. "In the phone message I got off the guy's phone. EZ and numbers. Could that be a Bible verse? EZ for Ezekiel?"

Ira's magnificent eyebrows went up. "That's quite a theory."

"Check it out," I said.

Ira tapped his keyboard and brought my picture of the message up on the screen. EZ was clearly seen. The number 28 was readable, the last numbers fuzzy. Ira zoomed in.

"Looks to me like 2812," Ira said.

"Could it be Ezekiel 28:12?"

"Why don't we look?" Ira said. He brought up the verse on the screen.

Son of man, take up a lament concerning the king of Tyre and say to him: This is what the Sovereign Lord says: You were the seal of perfection, full of wisdom and perfect in beauty.

"So?" I said.

Ira turned his wheelchair toward me. "By Jove, I think you've got it."

"Got what?"

"It. Prepare to be thunderstruck."

"Bring it," I said.

"A lament about the King of Tyre," Ira said. "In which the King of Tyre is a stand-in for Lucifer. This is a section about the pride of Lucifer and his fall from Eden."

"I thought he fell from Heaven," I said.

"It says he was the guardian cherub over Eden."

"I thought he was a snake in the grass."

"This is before Adam. Way before."

"You're going to have to explain that one to me," I said.

"The first two verses of Genesis," Ira said. "In the beginning, God created the heavens and the earth. But the earth became a formless void. In Hebrew the word sometimes translated *was* can also be *became.* And formless and void in Hebrew are *tohu wa-bohu.* Those words used together are always used as a state of being cursed."

"I'm confused," I said. "God creates a cursed earth?"

"No. The earth *became* cursed. Why? Because the earth was to be overseen by the guardian cherub, Lucifer. But when he rebelled, God brought a curse upon the earth. It is dark and covered with water. In the Hebrew scriptures, those words, *darkness* and *deep*, are negative terms. It is out of that watery darkness and chaos that God brings forth the earth of Genesis. What he did was take the earth away from Lucifer and gave dominion to Adam. That's why Lucifer shows up as a serpent and tempts Eve and Adam to rebel. His whole program is to destroy mankind and bring it over to, as the movies would say, the dark side."

"Mission accomplished," I said.

"It's not over yet," Ira said.

I said, "So a guy who identifies with Lucifer is communicating with Elliott's bodyguard. Could be Elliott himself. He could have texted his man after we walked out."

"That would make some sense," Ira said, "considering Elliott's profile."

"Does any of this make sense?"

"It's not supposed to make sense," Ira said.

"What?"

"Satan hides in confusion and chaos. He's got his own *tohu wa-bohu* program."

My phone buzzed. Coltrane Smith calling me back. I went outside to take the call.

"What can I do for you, Mr. Romeo?"

"You can put me in witness protection and provide for my needs for the rest of my life."

"Let me work on that. Anything else?"

"I need some help identifying a guy."

"Does this have anything to do with your current legal troubles?"

"Haven't you heard? I have no legal troubles. The District Attorney's office has made the reasonable decision to withdraw their complaint."

"Well, that's certainly good news."

"I think I have a lead on the guy who really did it."

"Knifed Tatum Walker?"

"Uh-huh."

"Isn't this something for us to handle?"

"I'm going to stifle a snort," I said.

"Mike, you know what I mean."

"There are too many spinning plates," I said.

"Have you spoken to the detective in charge? Who is it?"

"Meyer."

"Yeah, Meyer. He's good."

"He wants me to help him in any way I can."

"He told you that?"

"Not in so many words."

"What words did he use?"

"Well, he asked me not to muck around."

"And that sounds like asking you for help?"

"I interpret sounds different ways," I said. "You should hear me with birds."

"Mike, listen—"

"You know me, Cole. You know I wouldn't ask if I didn't have something, and if I didn't need it."

"I interpret your needs in different ways," he said.

"Fair enough," I said. "Can I send you a picture of the guy?"

"Who is it?"

"He's a bodyguard for Weston Elliott."

"Where have I heard that name?"

"He's a galloping atheist, leads a group called the O'Hair Society."

"What's his connection to your case?"

"He might be behind the attack. He's made a lot of noise about Walker."

"How do you know about his bodyguard?"

"I had a little chat with them both at the reading room they have downtown."

"Chatted?"

"The bodyguard didn't say much, but he did escort me out of the room."

"Why don't you tell all this to Meyer?"

"He'd think I was mucking about."

"You are."

"But I have a feeling about this. If they know Meyer's looking at them, it may let them slip away, and they may do more damage before they go."

"Mike, let us handle this."

I got hot. "I'm not some clown, man. I've got a missing client, I've got a charge still hanging over me. Meyer hasn't told me I'm scot-free. The DA can refile. And I'm tired of running into cul-de-sacs. You going to help me out or not?"

"Send me the picture."

"You're a prince among men."

"Don't overdo it," he said.

B ack inside I told Ira I needed to punch a side of beef or go for a run. He recommended the latter.

I got in some togs and took off on a familiar path. Back when I was living with Ira I used to run these neighborhoods. I ran past the Catholic church where a bomb went off a few years ago. Things looked back to normal, with children laughing in a play area. Good for them, laugh while you can.

I ran the sidewalk down Franklin. Had to avoid a few tents, a woman with a stuffed shopping cart, and an overzealous Lexus while crossing Bronson. I took a right on Beechwood and headed toward the hills. This is the street a lot of people use to get a view of the Hollywood sign. Tourists from Des Moines and Tokyo, Tulsa and Luxembourg, they see it and ooh and ahh and take a bunch of selfies.

Why? What does the Hollywood sign mean anymore? It had glamour once, when Cary Grant and Bette Davis and Bogart and Bacall were around making movies people actually wanted to see. Now movie houses were closing down because mass audiences don't want to pay twenty bucks for the four hundredth Marvel movie, or another iteration of the ruined Star Wars franchise, or the next hectoring social commentary in the thin disguise of a story.

I wound my way back to Los Feliz Boulevard and got to Ira's with a nice sweat. I took a shower and ran cold water the last minute. I got dressed and checked my phone. Coltrane Smith had called me. I called back.

"Your guy might be Hector De León. I stress may be. Parolee. Did a nickel at Corcoran for manslaughter."

"Maybe I should talk to his P.O."

"About what? What's he done?"

"I'm not sure. Yet."

"Then there's no point. A parole officer isn't going to give you squat."

"Okay then," I said. "Just tell me where De León lives and I'll interview him myself."

"Ha ha."

"Not going to tell me?"

"Goodbye, Mike. Stay cool."

He cut the call.

I went back in the house.

"Ira?"

"Yes?"

"I need you to find me an address for a parolee named Hector De León."

Ira Rosen went into action. I took down a book and flipped through it while he worked. It was a book of verse. I came to

Matthew Arnold's poem, "Dover Beach." That brought back
memories. I had to do a paper on it when I was at Yale. The
big question scholars have is whether it's a dark or hopeful
poem. I landed on the dark side then, because I didn't see any
great love heading my way. I wondered if I'd changed.

I read the last stanza.

Ah, love, let us be true
To one another! for the world, which seems
To lie before us like a land of dreams,
So various, so beautiful, so new,
Hath really neither joy, nor love, nor light,
Nor certitude, nor peace, nor help for pain;
And we are here as on a darkling plain
Swept with confused alarms of struggle and flight,
Where ignorant armies clash by night.

We're on a darkling plain for sure. But can we make it
beautiful if we have love?

Sophie…

"This your guy?" Ira said.

I clapped the book shut and put it back on the shelf. I went
to the monitor and looked at a mug shot.

"Put shades on him and he could definitely be Elliott's
bodyguard," I said.

"Could be?"

"Close enough. Where's he live?"

"What are you going to do?"

"Just have a look," I said.

"You never just have a look."

"I'm not going to not look, Ira. I'm getting sick of running
into walls."

"You've done some severe damage to walls."

"I'm not going to sit around," I said. "If I do I'll start
breaking stuff."

"Don't do anything until I tell you," Ira said.

In an Igor voice, I said, "Yes, master."

"Oy gevalt."

Ira started tickling the keyboard.

I took another book off his shelf. A volume of William Blake's poetry. Interesting cat, Blake. Engraver, painter, poet who had visions, lots of visions, of angels and devils and even his own dead brother. I read a couple of his short poems, and then eyes my landed on this—

Love seeketh not itself to please,
Nor for itself hath any care,
But for another gives its ease,
And builds a heaven in hell's despair.

Oh man. That thought was digging into my brain when Ira said, "Found it."

He had a street maps location on the monitor. It was through an open, wrought-iron gate. Several old, squat, dilapidated houses. A tarp-covered parking area on one side. Ira pointed to one of the houses. "That would be the one."

"Pleasant."

"It's in Boyle Heights, near the Evergreen Cemetery."

"So how do I get a look without ending up in the cemetery myself?"

Ira moved the picture. "It's an alley access. That doesn't afford you much cover. Wait."

He turned the view 180. There was a cinder block wall and barbed wire on top. But the cement lot on the other side was empty.

"That might offer a vantage point," Ira said.

"I'll check it out," I said. "After my nap."

I t was almost dark when I got to Boyle Heights. On the blocks near the cemetery the houses had bars on the windows, cracks in the sidewalk, not many people walking the streets. According to Ira, there are thirty Hispanic gangs active in Boyle Heights, mostly named after their streets of residence. A fine place for me to be spotted. Which is why I wasn't wearing a loud Tommy Bahama, but a black sweatshirt, black jeans, and black shoes, with a dark blue knit cap. Romeo the ninja.

I drove around until it was fully dark, then drove to the empty lot opposite De León's crib.

It was fenced, gated and padlocked.

The good thing was there were no lights. No signs, either. It appeared to have been a parking lot. Maybe for a defunct business, or even a church.

There weren't any people around, so I got out and examined the padlock. A simple one, which I picked in thirty seconds. I opened the gate enough to drive in with headlights off.

Once inside, I closed the gate and replaced the lock without clicking it.

Then I drove to the far corner. I'd brought the gun I'd lifted from the protections guy. I got out, put the gun in my waistband, and looked over the wall and through the barbed wire. There was the alley, and dimly lit by interior lights the place where De León was supposed to hang.

And what would I do if I saw him?

My plans were, as they say, flexible.

The sound of hip-hop filled the air.

This was to be my soundtrack for the next hour. There was a small gate in the corner, also locked. I picked it.

Surveillance is waiting, mostly boring, and mentally tiring. I once went on a sit with Joey Feint that lasted five hours without a significant sight. Our mark finally showed up, a skip trace, and before Joey nabbed him, he said, "You don't get the gold if you give up the dig."

But then something interesting happened.

An SUV came down the alley and turned into the lot where De León's pad was. It cruised right up to it, stopped, and a guy got out, went to the door, and knocked.

A second later the door opened. From the back light inside the house I couldn't tell if it was De León who did the opening. There was a quick exchange. Classic drug buy. The driver got back in the Escalade and backed out of the lot, then headed down the alley and away.

Business as usual in Los Angeles.

A black sedan came next. It pulled up next to the house just beyond De León's. All the doors opened and five guys and a woman–presumably–poured out. They were laughing and chatting it up. In Spanish.

They laughed up to the door. One of the guys unlocked it and they all went in.

Fifteen minutes went by without much activity. Somebody drove by the entrance to the court, stopped, idled. I instantly thought, drive-by. It happens a lot more than is reported by the media. Wouldn't want to give the city a reputation, now would we?

But no shots were fired and the car drove on.

So what did I have? De León was dealing drugs. Had a cartel or hardcore gang connection, or maybe was selling little units as a solo. Just like a kid with a lemonade stand.

So was Elliott in on it? Or was De León moonlighting, as it were? Bodyguard by day, drug dealer by night?

Something moved along the wall a foot from my face.

I jumped back.

It was a rat. A big rat. It hissed. Get out of my house, it was saying.

I hissed back.

The rat scurried away.

Romeo 1, vermin 0.

That would go on my resume.

The minutes dragged by. The house party got louder. Could be a meth take, or Ecstasy boost. Or maybe just old-school tequila shooters. A good time had by all. Until the morning.

Another car rolled in, stopped at De León's. A guy got out, looked at his phone. Waited.

The door opened. Another exchange. They talked for a few seconds. Then the guy drove off.

This could go on all night.

I probably had enough to be a confidential informant. Maybe enough to get Coltrane Smith interested in serving a warrant. But for something this low level the cops might skip it. Getting street dealers is only worth it if they turn on their sources, and that was hard to do without a major crime hanging over them. Even then it might not happen, as informers don't last long on the street or in prison.

I probably wasn't going to get much more, even following the Yogi Berra advice—*You can observe a lot just by watching.*

I gave myself another half hour.

A police helicopter chopped by, maybe a mile away. Did some circling. Sirens sounded in the distance. The urban symphony. The whole city was a concert hall now, including the suburbs. Even upper crust enclaves like Calabasas and Porter Ranch had performances.

And the band played on.

It was near my half-hour cutoff that I got a break

De León came out, closed the door, and checked it. Then used a key to lock a deadbolt.

He was wearing a hoodie, went to the parking spots. He got in an SUV, backed out, and drove to the alley.

Toward me.

I ducked behind the wall and listened until it went by. I caught the taillights as they disappeared.

Now or never.

Never is not an option for me.

I went through the gate, watched the courtyard, then ran to the side of the door. Put my back to it and drew my weapon.

Knocked.

Waited.

Knocked again.

I checked the door. Locked, and there was a bolt.

The door lock was no problem. My break was that he'd locked the bolt from the outside, with a key. That meant it could be picked.

I picked it. And went inside, closing and locking the door behind me. The smell of grilled peppers and baked weed was heavy in the air.

The windows were blacked out. I used my phone flashlight to scan the room. Couch, some chairs, and a table with a digital scale on it. Next to the scale was a little pile of dime baggies and some pieces of tin foil. And a pipe and baggie of marijuana.

Not much else to the room.

I made my way to the hallway. There was an open door to

a bathroom that looked like it hadn't been cleaned since Obama left office. The stink was thick.

There were two more doors. One was open. All that was in it was a mattress and some trash. The walls were a tagger's canvas, gang symbols, words in Spanish, and names.

And there, right in the middle, a devil's head, with horns and a smile. This was not the land of subtle.

The other door was closed. I tried the knob. Locked.

I put my ear to the door. It wasn't easy, as the music at the next-door party was pumping.

But I'd come this far.

I picked the lock, then threw the door open, keeping to the side, outside the door, with my gun in hand.

After a few seconds, I used the phone flashlight to look in the room.

Empty except for one item. A bed in the corner. An actual bed with an iron frame.

And someone in the bed handcuffed to the frame.

He wasn't moving. His skeletal arm hung from the cuffs, his hand folded over like a dead fish. And he was completely naked.

I approached slowly, even though this guy wasn't going to make any sudden moves. He was clearly some poor sap who was being held and maybe tortured for some drug deal gone bad.

I shined the light on his face.

It was the nervous tic guy from Sonhouse.

It didn't matter if he was dead or alive. I had to get him out of there. Now.

I picked the cuffs and put his arms over his chest. His body wasn't cold, a good sign.

There was a blanket bunched up on the floor. I spread it out.

Then picked Tic up off the bed. He weighed less than a

hundred pounds by my quick calculation. I put him on the blanket and wrapped it around him.

"Can you hear me?" I said.

His eyelids fluttered. He moaned. It wasn't much, but it was a sign he was holding on to life.

"Hang on. I'm going to get you help."

I picked him up off the floor, carried him to the front room.

Then I put him over my shoulder like a sailor's duffel.

I opened the door a crack and looked out.

No one in the lot that I could see.

Party still happening next door.

I figured ten seconds to get to the gate and my car.

I figured wrong.

I made a quick move across the courtyard toward the parking area. My one advantage was the darkness. An advantage that lasted two seconds. Headlights flashed into the alley, coming my way. If I tried to get to the gate, I'd be like the proverbial deer caught in the headlights, only one who was carrying another deer on his shoulders.

I ducked back between two cars under the awning, crouched down. The headlights turned into the courtyard and drove past me up to De León's house. A guy got out and went to the door. He knocked. Waited. Knocked again. He took out his phone and it looked like he was tapping out a text.

Tic, still on my shoulder, groaned. The party noise was ambient enough to drown him out. But I wasn't taking any chances. I cooed at him like he was a restless baby. Some things you never think you'll do, ever, until circumstances force it on you. Nursemaid Romeo.

The guy got mad. He pounded on the door. Desperate for a fix, no doubt.

Finally, he got back in his idling car and burned rubber out of there.

Just as more light spilled into the courtyard. Because a party animal staggered outside the house. He was laughing and shouting something in Spanish.

Tic moaned.

I cooed.

Still laughing, the guy shuffled toward my position. From the backlight out of the house I could see he wasn't too big.

He was certainly loud enough to make a lot of noise if he saw something he didn't like.

Like me.

He came closer.

My head was low and I could see him advance, until he veered off. I lost sight of him then because of the car parked on my right.

I waited a beat, then allowed myself to rise a bit to see where he was.

He was one car over. Looking down.

At what?

I ducked back down. I was going to have to make a move before more partiers spilled out or cars came in.

There was a momentary lull in the music. Which made it possible to hear the steady stream one car over, and I knew then what the guy was doing.

He took a long time doing it.

Somebody shouted, "Miguel!"

The guy in midstream said, "Cállate!"

And they both laughed.

It seemed like half an hour for the waterfall to stop. Now the guy could head back and I could head out.

But he didn't head back.

There was a flash of light, like from a lighter. A few seconds later I sniffed the skunk-sweet smell of ganja.

The guy was blunting and not in any hurry to share with his compadres.

Tic let out a wail.

"Hey," the guy said. "What goes?"

There are only two things to do when you're made. Run away like mad or lean into it and change the circumstances. Running was out.

So I said, "Help."

The shadowy form came round the car on my right and stood there.

"Help me, man, I'm hurt," I said.

He moved forward. If he hadn't been high he might have used more street caution.

Instead, he leaned over.

With my right hand I grabbed his shirt and yanked him down.

He cursed in his native tongue.

I clocked him. Down he went. Poor guy, all he wanted was to party. What he got was concussed.

My feeling of sympathy lasted half a second.

I got up and carried Tic to the gate, opened it, and put him in the back seat of Spinoza. I drove to the front gate, got out, threw it open, and shot into the street.

Finding the freeway was like being liberated from prison.

I called Artra.

"Mike, what is it?"

"I've got a guy here," I said. "I think he's been drugged. He's a witness. I don't want to take him to a hospital. Can you take a look at him?"

"Of course. Where are you?"

"I'm on the 10, heading home. Traffic's not bad so far."

"Meet me at the clinic."

"I'll be there."

There was some slowing on PCH at Santa Monica. The night air was crisp.

My package in the back was moaning steady.

"You're gonna be all right," I said.

"Help, help." His voice was weak.

"Stay cool. You're safe."

He was silent after that.

Artra was waiting outside the clinic with a gurney.

I stopped in front of her. I got out and pulled Tic up to a sitting position, then lifted him out and put him on the gurney.

Artra opened the door and I pushed him in.

"This way," she said.

I followed her down a hallway into an observation room.

"What do you know?" she said.

"What you see," I said.

"What's his name?" Artra said.

"I don't know."

Arta pulled his eyelids. "Can you hear me?"

"Uh . . ."

Artra attached a BP cuff to his arm and a clip to his index finger. The monitor beeped and showed heart rate.

"I'm going to give him Naloxone," Artra said.

She took a spray thing out of a box.

"Lift him slightly," she said.

I did.

She put her hand under his neck and pushed his head back slightly.

"Hang on," she said. "This'll help."

She put the nozzle in one of his nostrils and thumbed the plunger.

Tic stiffened, chuffed.

"Easy now," Artra said. "You just rest." She got a fresh blanket from a cabinet and laid it over him.

"When can I talk to him?" I said.

"I'm going to be with him awhile," Artra said. "Why don't you wait in my office? It's at the end of the hall. I'll let you know."

A rtra Murray's office was a cramped but neat space, with one bookshelf of medical texts and journals, and a filing cabinet. Her desk had a laptop and papers on either side. What was noticeable was a lack of the usual framed diplomas and commendations you usually find on the walls. The only adornment was a photograph of a good-looking young Marine in dress blues.

I remembered she had a son who died in combat during the first battle of Fallujah in Iraq.

I felt like saluting the picture. So I did.

As is my wont, I took a random book from the shelf and sat in a chair. I flipped it open to a random page and found a heading on The Krebs Cycle. It explained that this is a chain reaction in the mitochondria that enables cells to produce energy.

Fairly important. I read the article until I got to oxidative phosphorylation, and then gave up.

It was late, but Ira needed to know. I called him.

His voice was sleepy. "What's wrong, Michael?"

"I got into De León's place," I said. "I found a guy there, from Sonhouse, shackled and drugged out of his mind."

"Where are you now?"

"Dr. Murray's clinic on PCH. She's taking care of him. He may be able to talk soon."

"I should be there," Ira said.

"Wait till tomorrow. Let him recover."

"Are you all right?"

"All things considered," I said.

"And what does that mean?"

"Tomorrow, Ira. Get some sleep."

"Ha."

H alf an hour later, Artra came to the office.

"He's stable," she said. "But undernourished and dehydrated. What happened to the poor guy?"

"Not sure," I said. "Found him in a drug house, cuffed to a bed."

"Dear God."

"Can I talk to him?"

"Oh, Mike—"

"Just for a minute."

"Keep it short," Arta said.

T ic, hooked up to an IV drip, said, "You!"

"Don't be afraid," I said. "You've got the finest doctor in the country looking after you."

He looked at Artra. "Thank you," he said.

She smiled. "You've got a good friend here."

"What's your name?" I said.

He hesitated.

"I'm Mike," I said.

"Alvin," he said.

I said, "What can you tell us, Alvin?"

He frowned. Looked like he was trying to put scrambled thoughts together.

Then he screamed. "The devil! He'll kill me!"

"Whoa, hold on there," I said.

"Don't let him! Help!"

Artra put her hand on his cheek. "Alvin, easy now. You're safe. No devil here. God is here. You understand?"

Alvin blinked a few times. "Really?"

"Really," Arta said. "Nothing can get past God."

He closed his eyes. Labored breath infused his skinny body. Artra stroked his hair.

Then he opened his eyes. And started to cry.

"That's enough for now," Arta said to me.

"Mike," Alvin said, tears flowing now.

"I'm here," I said.

"Mike, Mike . . . I killed him!"

"What do you mean?" I said.

"Reverend Walker," Alvin said. "I cut his throat!"

He began to wail. His body shook like a flag in the wind. Artra pushed me aside, saying, "Go outside, Mike."

She bent over Alvin, started calming him down.

I backed out of the room.

I called Ira.

"Still awake?" I said.

"I'm having tea," He said.

"Well, put down your cup. This guy just copped to cutting Walker's throat."

I heard the hard clink of china hitting china. "What did you just say?"

"He thinks he killed him," I said.

"Are you sure?"

"If the words I killed him, I cut his throat have any meaning, then yes. There's the connection."

"Explain."

"De León had him. He was drugged. He was pumped up and put up to the attack by Elliott."

"He told you that?"

"Actually, no. He's a bit upset."

"I'm coming," Ira said.

W hen he got there, Alvin was sitting up, eating applesauce. Artra allowed us to talk to him.

"How you feeling?" I said.

With a hangdog look, Alvin said, "I wish I was dead."

"None of that," I said. "Can you tell us what happened?"

"I don't want to," he said. "I just want to die."

"No, you don't," I said. "Now, try."

"If you can," Artra said.

"You can," I said.

"Take your time," Ira said.

"It's all fuzzy," Alvin said. "They shot me up."

"Who shot you up?" I said.

"I don't know. I was in a room, a little room."

"How many people were there?" Ira said.

Alvin closed his eyes. "I can't remember."

"More than one?"

"Yeah... yeah..." He opened his eyes. They were full of fear. "The devil was there!"

He dropped his applesauce and covered his face with his hands.

"All right," Artra said. "That's enough for now. Let him get some strength."

"One more question," I said to Artra. "Okay?"

"One more," she said.

I brought up a picture of Weston Elliott on my phone.

"Alvin, do you recognize this guy?"

Slowly, Alvin lowered his hands and looked. Shook his head. Then said, "Mask."

"He wore a mask?"

"Yeah, yeah."

"What kind of mask?"

His face twisted in pain.

Artra said, "That's enough, Mike."

"We're just getting somewhere," I said.

"You're getting out," Artra said.

I ra and I went out to the reception area.

"Do we have to report this?" I said.

Ira thought about it, then, "No."

"Really?"

"Right now he's my client," Ira said.

"He just confessed."

"I am not the police. I am not obligated to report anything, unless I am convinced a client is about to commit a crime. Besides, considering his mental state, we don't know the value of his statement. I once had a client who insisted he committed a crime he was clearly innocent of."

"Why would he do that?"

"He wanted three hots and a cot. He found life outside of prison intolerable. We don't know what's in Alvin's mind right now. We give him time. Then we do some negotiating, maybe get him diverted for his treatment."

"In that case," I said. "Can we eat something?"

I drove to a place on PCH that makes meaty breakfast burritos. I brought three back. We sat with Artra in her office. She'd made the coffee.

"What can you tell me about this case?" Artra asked.

"You tell her," Ira said.

I launched into it, starting with Coby and Zon and Lucifer is coming, and ending with the incident at De León's.

When I finished, Artra said, "Never a dull moment with you, Mike."

"Amen to that," Ira said.

"May I share a theory?" she said.

"Please," Ira said.

"I'm not saying this is such a case, at least not yet. But I suspect he's been subjected to a psychoactive drug, LSD or MDMA. And there's a newer one, out of Colombia, called burundanga. Otherwise known as scopolamine. It's nasty. It can take away free will. In the right hands, or I should say the wrong hands, it can be used to turn somebody into a puppet, open to suggestion to do very bad things."

"That's been known to happen," Ira said.

"When?" I said.

"The Manson family," Ira said.

"And do you know what the street name for this drug is?" Artra said.

"I do not," said Ira.

"The Devil's Breath," Artra said.

You could have heard a pitchfork drop.

"That," I said, "explains a lot."

"It's just a theory," Artra said. "We'll know more after a tox screen. But I caution you, scopolamine interferes with acetylcholine, a neurotransmitter essential to memory. There's a likelihood Alvin won't remember a lot of what happened to him."

"Would you be our expert witness?" Ira said.

"Of course," Artra said. "Temporary insanity?"

"Not exactly," Ira said. "Evidence of involuntary intoxica-tion can be considered in deciding whether a defendant had the capacity to form the specific intent necessary for the crime charged."

"So, diminished capacity," Artra said.

"They don't call it that in California anymore," Ira said. "But the idea is the same."

"I'll be there when you need me," Artra said.

Outside the clinic, the morning sun was breaking through the marine layer.

"What now, boss?" I said.

"Why don't you see if you can talk to Tatum Walker?" Ira said. "He needs to hear all this. If a police presence is there, you know what to do."

"Use my charm?"

"Good heavens, no. Give them one of my cards and make it official."

"Not as fun," I said. "But I'll try."

There was no police presence, but there was something just as impenetrable—a head nurse who looked like she'd last smiled in the Clinton administration. So I used both Ira's card and, yes, my charm. It was probably the card that did it, but the nurse talked to Walker, then said I could go in for a few minutes, as long as I didn't have him talk too much.

He was sitting up in the bed. His neck was heavily bandaged. An open Bible was on his lap and on the table next to him was a spray of flowers and a big *Get Well Soon* card.

Smiling, he stuck out his hand. His grip was strong. He mouthed, "Thank you for coming."

"How you doing?" I said.

He gave me a thumbs up. Then picked up the Bible and pointed to a verse. It was underlined. *But he was wounded for*

our transgressions, he was bruised for our iniquities: the chas-
tisement of our peace was upon him; and with his stripes we
are healed.

"There are a few things you need to know," I said.
"Ready?"

He nodded.

"A guy from Sonhouse, Alvin. Know him?"

Softly, Tatum said, "Sure."

"I found him in a drug house, almost dead. I got him to a
clinic run by a doctor friend. She's brought him around. He
says he's the one, the one who cut you."

Tatum frowned.

I said, "Did he have something against you?"

Tatum shook his head.

"He saw me at Sonhouse a couple days ago, thought I was
the devil. The place I found Alvin was a drug house for sure,
and had a wall with a big devil's head painted on it. Whole lot
of devil around."

Tatum motioned for me to lean closer. "I told you that,
remember?"

"I do."

"Will you turn Alvin in?"

"Ira is representing him. He'll make sure he's healthy
first."

"He needs help," Tatum said. "I'll testify to that."

"You don't think he's dangerous?"

"Drugged, anybody can snap. That's why he needs help."
He put his hand on my arm. "Did you find Coby?"

"Still looking," I said.

"I'm praying for you, brother," Tatum said. "God knows a
way where there is no way."

The nurse came back in.

"Time's up," she said.

"She's the boss," Tatum said.

"You got that right," said the nurse.

D riving away from the hospital was a dismal experience. The air was hot and sticky and full of fumes. All I wanted to do was get back to the Cove and go swimming.

But as I came down the California Incline toward PCH, Arta called me.

"You better get over here," she said.

"What's wrong?"

"Alvin keeps screaming he has to talk to you. I'm doing my best to keep him quiet."

In the background I heard Alvin's voice. "New moon sacrifice!"

"I'll be right over," I said.

T here were several people in the waiting area. Connie the receptionist took me to the back room where Artra was standing over the bedded Alvin.

The moment I walked in, he sat up straight, as if pushed by an unseen hand.

"You gotta listen!" His eyes were shiny and red-rimmed. "The devil, man. Sacrifice!"

"All right," I said. "Take it easy."

"There will be blood!"

Artra said, "Explain to your client that if he doesn't quiet down I'm going to sedate him and ship him out of here."

"What's that mean?" Alvin said.

I put my finger in front of his face. "It means you keep your voice down or I can't help you."

He got sheepish then. But a frightened sheep. "I'm scared, man. The devil wants me."

"The devil can't touch you," Artra said. "God rules here."

"That right?" Alvin asked me.

"If she says it, it's right," I said. "Now, quietly, what are you trying to tell me?"

"Guys talking," Alvin said. "Said there's gonna be a new moon sacrifice."

"Who's they?"

"I don't know. One guy had a mask on. The other guy was big. It was all fuzzy."

"They pumped you up," I said.

"Yeah, yeah! I got it from behind."

"How'd it happen?"

"I don't know. It was dark. I was outside."

His eyes searched the ceiling.

"What else can you tell me?" I said.

He brought his eyes back to me. "Red temple," he said.

"Red temple?"

He nodded. "By the freeway."

"Where?"

"I seen it." His eyes got wild again. "Don't let him take me!"

"Listen to me, Alvin," I said. "Nobody's going to take you. You've got the best doctor, the best lawyer, and the best…"

"Enforcer?" Artra said.

"That'll do," I said. I put my finger in Alvin's face again. "Now, can you keep quiet?"

He nodded.

I went outside and called Ira.

"Alvin started ranting about a new moon sacrifice, maybe somewhere downtown. Talked about a red temple. Says he heard it from whoever drugged him."

"New moon sacrifice?" Ira said. "Are you sure about that?"

"Those were his exact words," I said.

Pause.

"Michael, in Jewish tradition, the New Moon, or Rosh Chodesh, is significant. It's a time for renewal and reflection. During the time of the Babylonian captivity, it was accompanied by a ceremony of blood sacrifice."

"Whoa."

"A priest would go outside Jerusalem and wave a long torch on the Mount of Olives. That would be seen by others, who would do the same on other hilltops. The signal would be transmitted all the way to Babylon. It was a sign of God's protective favor."

"I don't think Alvin had that in mind."

"Stay with me," Ira said. "Like many things, this ceremony was perverted by the enemies of God, especially those practicing the occult. The new moon is the absence of light. The forces of darkness believe they can at that time operate without interference from the divine. It is a time to call upon evil spirits and demonic powers. So the thinking goes."

"Even now?"

"It would appear so."

"With a sacrifice?"

"Exactly."

"Animal?"

"It doesn't sound like that here," Ira said. "It sounds like Alvin was being prepared for it."

"But he's out."

"They may procure another, and soon."

"Why do you say that?"

"Because Rosh Chodesh is tomorrow night."

I told Artra I wanted to take Alvin for a ride, then I'd park him at Ira's for the time being.

Artra said, "He's going to be sketchy for a while. Hard to

say how much. He's weak physically so he needs to eat and stay hydrated. He's likely to have mood swings, so be ready for that. He could get very depressed. I'll give you some Clondine tabs if his symptoms become severe. And get him into NA. I know it's a lot, but I also know you're the man for the job."

I wasn't so sure as I drove away with a nervous Alvin next to me. To keep him calm, I tried making conversation.

"Where you from, Alvin?"

"Nashville."

"Rockin' country."

"Yeah." He got a jolt of energy. "I was gonna be a songwriter."

"For real?"

"Next Dean Dillon."

"Don't know him," I said.

"Oh man! I'm Into the Bottle to Get You Out of My Mind. Genius. I saw him in concert. I wrote a song shoulda sold. You wanna hear it?"

"Maybe later," I said.

He started singing. "You're the train on my one-track mind, but baby I'm a nervous wreck—"

"Didn't sell, huh?" I said.

"What're you gonna do? Came out to L.A., nothing. Got hooked. Almost died. Tatum took me in…" He put his head in his hands. "They made me do it! I was out of my head!"

"All right, Alvin, all right. But we can maybe save a guy, if you work with me."

"What're we gonna do?"

"Find the red temple."

"I don't want to!"

"You want to make up for it, don't you?"

"Make up for what?"

"Tatum."

He cursed, low and hard.

"Listen to me, Alvin. Life is a series of mess ups. It's what you do with them that counts. You got to put some effort into it. You got to stand up. Can you do that for me?"

"What's gonna happen to me? I mean, with the cops."

"We'll figure that out later, okay?"

"I'm scared, man."

"That's life, too. Everybody's scared. The thing is to keep going anyway. If you walk up to fear and spit in its eye, it runs away like a punk."

"How do you know?"

"I've been doing a lot of spitting lately."

W e talked about a few other things. Alvin used to be into baseball. He was a Braves fan.

"Tommy Glavine, Greg Maddux, John Smoltz," he said. "I mean, come on!"

That got me talking about the Red Sox, and things were pleasant along the freeway until I pulled off at Hill Street. As we descended into downtown, Alvin got jittery. He kept looking around, as if he expected somebody to jump in the car and strangle him.

"Any idea which way to go?" I said.

"Maybe that way." Alvin pointed. "But I don't want to go that way."

"What if that's the way to go?"

"Oh man."

"Remember, spit."

"Okay," Alvin said. "That way."

.   .   .

P art of downtown is a grid. Numbered streets crossing named streets like Hill, Main, Broadway, Spring. We were at the top of Skid Row, Third and South Central Avenue. Alvin was biting his thumb sideways, like a dog with a bone.

"Right direction?" I said.

"I don't know," Alvin said. "Maybe."

"Keep looking."

We crossed Alameda. We came to a section with warehouses and small factories from the World War II era and 1950s. Some of them were fenced off and boarded up. Others repurposed for commercial use and even living spaces. Large murals covered some of the street-facing facades. Graffiti was splattered on others.

Mixed in were what was supposed to be luxury lofts and apartments, set apart by clean lines, large glass windows, and metal accents. Ten years ago there was a big move for urban upgrade down here. A lot of young professionals bought in. The hope was that the blight would be gradually mitigated. Didn't happen.

Alvin said, "I think ... keep going that way."

We cruised down a street, all the way to where it ended. There it was fenced off, and we were in the shadow of the freeway overhead. It felt like the end of the world.

"This looks sort of like it," Alvin said. "The freeway..."

He turned and looked behind him.

And yelped.

"There!"

I turned. It was a five-story, red brick building. It had graffiti all over it and a fence around it.

"The red temple?" I said.

"Yeah! Now can we get out of here?"

"You sure it's this place?"

"Yeah, I said! Come on, man!"

"Spit, Alvin, spit."

He looked at me. Then turned and spit out the window.

"You'll get there," I said. I turned Spinoza around and we went back the way we came. With each passing block Alvin breathed a little easier.

"What happens to me now?" he said.

"We place you in protective custody," I said.

"What's that mean?"

"It means in the hands of your attorney, Ira Rosen, who will make sure you eat something good for you, and will advise you of the legalities involved."

"Maybe I can just go back to Nashville."

"And be a fugitive? You don't want that. That way leads back to the monkey. You're off drugs for good."

He didn't look convinced.

"Ira Rosen's chicken soup is the best thing for you," I said. "Cures all ills."

"For real?"

"Believe it," I said.

I took Wilshire instead of the freeway. I called Ira and told him we were on our way.

He was ready for us. He even had the chicken soup going.

We sat in the front room. Ira did his best to explain the legalities to Alvin. Alvin wiggled around in his chair. Then Ira had me serve up the soup. It calmed Alvin down some. I took him out back while Ira made some calls.

We sat on the bench under Ira's magnolia tree.

"This is nice," Alvin said.

"You can beat the street," I said.

He shook his head, then held his hands up. "Sometimes I don't feel like I got control over these. Like they got their own mind, you know?"

"We hold in our hands the power to end our sorrows," I said.

"Huh?"

"It's from an old play."

"You know a lot of that old stuff, don't you?" Alvin said.

"It's all sound and fury, signifying nothing, unless you put it to use."

"You going down there?" Alvin said.

"Where?"

"Red temple."

"Yes," I said.

"Oh man, don't do it."

"What did I just say? If we have the power to end sorrow, we have to use it."

He thought about it. "If I get clean . . . "

"When you get clean," I said.

"You know what I'm gonna do?"

"Tell me."

"I'm gonna write a song," he said. "About you."

"You'll have to find a good rhyme for Romeo."

He smiled. "Buffalo?"

"I'm sure it'll be quite a song," I said.

B ack inside, Ira informed us that Artra had arranged for a two-night stay at a rehab place in Inglewood. Ira said we could drive him there after four.

"You can drive him," I said.

"Me?" Ira said. "Where are you going?"

Alvin said, "The red temple."

"The what?" Ira said.

I told Ira what Alvin told me.

"That's not much to go on," Ira said.

"I'll just watch," I said. "Nothing else is happening."

"It will," Alvin said.

It did.

I t was around ten when I got downtown. I parked a block
away from the end of the world, the freeway overpass. I
walked the rest of the way. I was in my ninja togs and had my
gun. The sound of cars in the night was like ghosts flying
through a graveyard with a rustling of leaves and wind in the
trees. I sensed there were people down here, like rats hidden
in dark corners. Or maybe even real rats. The smell of
garbage and exhaust fumes was strong enough to roll up like
a carpet.

My eyes were adjusted to the dark and everything was
draped in gray or black. I saw a cement stanchion that would
make a good observation point. As I walked toward it I noticed
a pile of something ten feet away. I went over for a look. It was
clothes. At the top of the pile was what looked like a jacket.
That's when I heard the snort.

It came from under the clothes. A guy was asleep there. So
I wasn't going to be alone after all.

I took up my position behind the stanchion. The brick
building was fifty yards away, dark, no cars around. I knew
this could turn out to be one of those five-hour surveillances
that ends with a big load of nothing. That's about fifty percent
of stakeout results.

My mind wandered over to Sophie. I wondered if she was
sleeping soundly in her nice, warm bed. Or was she tossing
around thinking about other things, like where I might be and
whether I was about to be shot or stabbed or punched in the
face. She'd always be wondering about that, wouldn't she?
She'd be like a cop's wife. That's tough duty.

Twenty, thirty minutes went by. There was some car
activity up a block, but nothing down where I was. Until a car

came halfway down the street toward my position, and stopped, engine idling. It killed the headlights.

But a light came on in the car, through a tinted windshield. From the look of it, it was the light of a phone. It barely illuminated a head on the driver's side. Then went out.

The car sat there with a soft engine purr.

Then another car came slowly down and pulled alongside the first, and stopped. The headlights went off. Both drivers got out, went around and opened the trunks. I couldn't see what they were doing. It looked like the transfer of a package or bundle. The guy from the second car put whatever it was in his trunk and closed it. The two men talked for a second. Then they got in their cars and drove off.

Could have been a drug buy, or weapons. It wasn't office supplies or baby clothes. Just another of innumerable transactions made every night in the dark corners of the city.

That was it, until half an hour or so later. An SUV came down the same street as the other cars, shooting headlight beams my way. It turned right and stopped at the fence around the brick building. Somebody got out of the passenger side. Whoever it was had on a long coat with a hood. He unlocked the gate. Then threw it open. The SUV drove inside. The hood closed the gate, locked it, got back in the car. They drove up to the building.

It was hard to see what happened next. From where I was I only had a partial view. But I did see two people go into the building. I waited a minute, then walked slowly toward the fence. The SUV was not idling. I made a quick feel of the padlock on the gate. It was a serious lock. Maybe an ABUS Granit. Which meant picking it was out of the question unless I had more specialized tools. Which I didn't.

The only way in was over.

But there was barbed wire on top.

I went back to where the sleeping guy was and took the jacket off the pile. It was a foul-smelling thing, like it was laundered in gutter water and used as a mat at Jiffy Lube.

I tossed it over a section of wire. Then I went up and over, managing not to get stuck. I took out my gun and crept to the SUV. I determined it was empty. The door to the brick building was open a crack. I listened, heard nothing, pushed the door a little more.

Went inside.

I didn't dare put on a light. I stood in the shadows. Didn't sense any movement. I could see shapes, the way you do in the dark. I couldn't tell what, if anything, was on the floor. I slowly slid one foot forward, then the other, like I was in a minefield. Still couldn't hear anything.

Until somebody hocked a loogie. It came from a distance, and from above. I moved toward the sound until I came to a set of stairs. Metal stairs. Which was good. No creaking sound from wood like in the movies.

Up I went, slow and easy.

A guy cleared his throat. The sound echoed down. Was it the same guy?

The steps zigged as I got to the fourth floor.

There was a light at the top of the stairs.

Holding my piece at the ready, I took one step, then another.

And saw De León, in profile, leaning against the wall, looking at his phone.

I ran up the last steps. His head snapped up.

"Don't move," I said.

He moved.

Dropping the phone, he fumbled for something under his shirt.

Before he could get it, I charged and gave him a pistol whip to the head. He slumped but had enough in him to put a shoulder into my middle.

And then I was on my back with De León on top of me.

I dropped my gun so I could grab with both hands. If he knew what he was doing, he could have had me in a Kimura hold. But he was a street fighter. No skills. I locked his left arm and swept my leg over him, flipped him like a fish. I got on my knees and put my hands under his legs and flipped him again, this time over his head.

And down the stairs.

His head made a resonant thunk on the metallic steps, all the way to the bottom.

I followed, ready for him to move.

But he didn't move.

In fact, he was never going to move again.

I searched his body and removed his piece. I put it in my waistband.

Then I went back up, recovered my own gun.

There was a door. I pushed it open and saw another set of stairs. It went to another door.

Roof access.

I opened it.

There was some kind of illumination out there. It was a fire. A small one, right in the middle of the roof.

And the guy in the robe and hood. He had his back to me. His arms were spread out. He was chanting something to the sky.

I took a triangle stance with my gun.

"Don't move," I said.

He spun around. Backlit as he was, I couldn't see his face. But I could see the knife in his hand.

"Drop it," I said.

A grating wail, like a screech monkey in heat, poured out of his mouth.

I said, "Drop it or you're dead."

The screech stopped. Replaced by a low cackle that turned into a crazy, all-out howl.

He turned and ran.

"Stop!" I said.

He didn't. He ran to the edge and, arms akimbo, he screamed what sounded like, "Take me!"

And he was gone.

I went to the edge and looked down. Under the illumination of a distant streetlight, the unmoving form looked like an oil stain.

The fire snapped. I didn't want the building to burn so I went back to stomp on it. I was about to start when I saw something in the flames.

A cat. A poor, dead cat, blackened and burned.

What fresh hell was this? This went beyond using devil imagery to intimidate and influence a drug-addled mind. This was outright satanic worship.

I did what I could to stop the burn. It wasn't easy. Tennis shoes were not made for this.

But I got enough of it to feel like it would soon go cold.

Then I heard a moaning.

Somebody else was up here. About twenty feet away. Stepping closer, gun ready, I saw a prostrate body.

"Hey," I said.

Nothing.

"Can you hear me?"

A pathetic gurgle was the answer.

I took out my phone. I gave the roof a quick look with the flashlight.

Clear.

Then I looked at the body again to see if he was hurt. He was naked. His body had bruises.

And his face had a name.

"Coby," I said. "Can you hear me?"

Moaning.

I put my gun next to the other, knelt down and picked up Coby. I put him over my shoulder. I took him down the stairs to De León's body. I knelt and pat searched De León with my right hand. And found his keys. Then it was out to the front gate, unlocked it, and we were out in the street.

I went around the block to where the body from the roof was. It was face down. I grabbed a handful of robe and turned the body over.

The death mask of Nathan White looked up at me. His eyes were open. They had a look of horror.

"Hey!"

Some guy was stumbling toward me.

"Where's my jacket?"

I headed for my car.

"Hey!" This was followed by a mix of oaths and incoherent fillers that echoed through the deserted canyon of the street at the end of the world.

C oby was barely breathing. No time to drive him to Artra's. I looked up the nearest emergency room and took him there. I carried him in like a wounded soldier from a Civil War battlefield. The receiving nurse didn't hesitate getting him inside. I stayed with him until they had him in a bed and all hooked up and a doctor looked in on him.

I kept the facts to myself but told the doc to be on the

lookout for a psychoactive drug. The doc asked me how I knew about that. I told him I liked to read.

Then I went outside and called Ira.

When I need to know what to do, I always call Ira.

"Unbelievable," Ira said.

"My exact thought," I said.

"First thing is we call Detective Meyer. I'll do that in the morning. You want to come over and get some sleep?"

"I think I'll stay here," I said. "I don't want to lose Coby again."

I did manage a few Zs on a chair in the waiting room. I was jostled awake by a young woman in scrubs. Morning light filtered in through the windows.

"Sorry to disturb you," she said. "The young man you brought in, what is your relationship?"

"He's a client," I said.

"We need to know who'll be responsible for the bill."

I rubbed my eyes. "How about the Governor of California?"

"Excuse me?"

"Nevermind. I'll pay it."

"Do you have any clothing for him?"

"No."

"We can give him a hospital gown."

"Make it so," I said.

At eleven they brought Coby out in a wheelchair. He was weak but coherent. I got some instructions from a nurse.

They'd given him Jell-O. I paid the bill then wheeled Coby outside.

"Mike," he said.

"Yeah?"

"I was gonna die, wasn't I?"

"Your time's not up," I said.

"You saved my life."

I said, "It's okay now, kid. I'm going to take you out to the beach. Breathe some good ocean air. Dr. Murray's going to take care of you."

"Mike?"

"Yeah?"

"Can you stay with me?"

"I'll be close," I said.

O n the way I asked what had happened to him at Sonhouse. Like Alvin, his details were sketchy. He remembered going outside at night, at Nathan White's request, to bring in some boxes. He remembered being grabbed from behind. Then it was a blank until he woke up cuffed to a bed. The rest was a nightmare, only he didn't know how much of it was only a dream.

He couldn't say much more and I didn't press him. It was a little after one when we got to Artra's clinic. I knew he was going to be okay when I helped him out of my car and a breeze flapped his hospital gown. "I feel like a new man," he said. "Too bad the old one has my underwear."

I t took three weeks for things to get straightened out in the mind of the LAPD. They searched Nathan White's apartment and laptop. They found emails from EZ2812, and using IP tracing found out our mystery man was, indeed, Weston Elliott. He has a lot of explaining to do, but is tight-lipped as he sits in jail in Castaic, awaiting trial for conspiracy to commit murder.

That Nathan White had been so convincingly sincere on the surface was a shock to my system.

But not to Tatum Walker's. When I spoke to him about it back in his office—he was healing nicely—he said he was hurt, to be sure, but not shocked.

"It's the devil's way," he said. "The wolf in sheep's clothing. And devil worship, actual worship, is on the rise. It can raise up an army of Nathan Whites."

"How do you think Elliott got involved?"

"Not hard to figure," Tatum said. "I believe in divine appointments, Mike. God sets up meetings. But the devil does, too. He brings blind minds together. The Bible calls him the god of this world who hath blinded the minds of them which believe not. The final battle is on. And there ain't gonna be no cease fire. The devil is in a fury because he knows his time is short."

He paused. "You bring Coby and Alvin back here. I'm not going to let them be collateral damage in this war."

"Ira's working on that," I said.

"You're a good man, my brother."

"Ira's working on that, too."

On a lazy Tuesday afternoon I was finishing a roast beef sammy, when I got a knock at my screen door.

A big lifeguard type stood there. He was in shorts, flip flops and a Hawaiian shirt. It was almost like looking in a mirror, except he was about ten years younger.

"Help you?" I said.

"Someone would like to see you," he said.

"That's cryptic," I said. "You know what cryptic is?"

"Sure," he said.

"I don't like cryptic," I said.

"You'll want to see this guy."

"What's this guy's name?"

"Come on down to the beach."

"He's on the beach?"

"You'll see."

"I don't want to see," I said.

"You will," he said. "It has something to do with your bail."

Now I did want to see.

"You armed?" I said.

"No way," he said, and laughed. "I'm a big admirer of yours, Mr. Romeo. I'm not here to fight you. I'd lose. But I'd love to learn some of your moves. My name's Hunter."

"All right, Hunter. I was going to do my nails, but I suppose it can wait."

I walked down to the beach with him. He told me he was from Texas and came out hoping to break into movies. He was taking acting lessons and worked for this guy, the guy who wanted to see me, on the side.

When we hit the sand he said, "Look out there."

About half a mile out was a white yacht, shimmering in the sun. Hunter took out his phone and sent a text.

"Watch this," he said.

A few moments later, somebody on a jet ski hit the water off the yacht. He came zooming in, right up to the sand, and hopped off.

He had a big smile on his face.

"Hello, Mike," he said.

"Zane Donahue," I said. Donahue was a mover and shaker among the crowd that skirted the fine line between legal and illegal activities. Someone I'd had a few dealings with in the past.

"Like my entrance?" Donahue said.

"It had a certain panache," I said.

"See?" he said to Hunter. "Didn't I tell you he liked those big words?"

Hunter smiled.

"Last time we were together," Donahue said, "you showed up unannounced at my house. I thought I'd return the favor."

I said, "Am I to understand you're the one who bailed me out?"

"You understand right."

"You put up a hundred grand?"

"There was a side bet," he said. "I know Ernie Orsatti, the bondsman. We go back a long time. I bet him there'd be no trial, not even a prelim. I ended up five grand to the good."

"Quite a risk," I said.

"That's the kick of big time betting," Donahue said. "Besides, I knew you didn't do it, that the whole thing was bogus, that you'd figure it all out. You did, and now you owe me."

"Oh, I do? How's that work?"

"You're a man of honor," Donahue said. "I admire that, even though I myself find little use for it. I might need a man like you from time to time."

"What about young Hunter here?" I said.

"I want him to watch you," Donahue said. "And learn."

"I don't known, Zane. My plate is pretty full."

"Ah, yes. Word on the street is that a girl has landed the great Mike Romeo."

Unbelievable. "You're checking up on me?"

"I always check my investments," Donahue said.

"I'm all choked up," I said.

"I'll even let you use my boat."

And quite a boat it was. I'd been on his yacht before, when it was docked in Marina Del Rey. He called it *The Max Baer* because he lived in the house formerly owned by 1930s heavy-weight champion of the world.

"Just promise me you'll think about it," Donahue said.

"I'm always thinking."

"Good enough."

He went back to his jet ski, put it in the water, and took off toward *The Max Baer*.

"He's pretty good at exits, too," Hunter said.

Sophie came over the next day. We took beach chairs and an umbrella down to the sand and set ourselves up. A marine layer hovered over the Cove, bringing Pacific cool.

"You know," Sophie said, "this is the first really calm moment we've had in months."

"Godzilla could still rise from the sea," I said.

"It wouldn't surprise me. He'd probably be looking for you."

"And you're okay with that?" I said.

"Who wouldn't love to see you punching out Godzilla?" she said.

"That's all I needed to know."

"Oh?"

I picked up a handful of sand and let it trickle out.

"The sands of time," Sophie said.

"I'm thinking of the good thing I want," I said.

"Only one?"

I waited till all the sand was out and brushed my hands off. Then I pulled Sophie into my arms.

"The one I want most," I said.

AUTHOR'S NOTE

Many thanks for reading *Romeo's Fire*. I greatly appreciate it. Added appreciation would come if you would kindly leave a review on the Amazon site.

The Mike Romeo Thriller Series
(in order)
1. Romeo's Rules
2. Romeo's Way
3. Romeo's Hammer
4. Romeo's Fight
5. Romeo's Stand
6. Romeo's Town
7. Romeo's Rage
8. Romeo's Justice
9. Romeo's Fire

FREE BOOK

I'd like to offer you a free suspense novella, FRAMED. You can pick it up by going to my website: JamesScottBell.com. Navigate to the FREE BOOK page and follow the link. Enjoy!

MORE THRILLERS FROM JAMES SCOTT BELL

The Ty Buchanan Legal Thriller Series

#1 Try Dying
#2 Try Darkness
#3 Try Fear

"Part Michael Connelly and part Raymond Chandler, Bell has an excellent ear for dialogue and makes contemporary L.A. come alive. Deftly plotted, flawlessly executed, and compulsively readable. Bell takes his place as one of the top authors in the crowded suspense genre." - **Sheldon Siegel**, *New York Times* bestselling author

The Trials of Kit Shannon Historical Legal Thrillers

Book 1 - City of Angels
Book 2 - Angels Flight
Book 3 - Angel of Mercy
Book 4 - A Greater Glory
Book 5 - A Higher Justice

Book 6 - A Certain Truth

"With her shoulders squared and faith set high, Kit Shannon arrives in 1903 Los Angeles feeling a special calling to practice law ... Packed full of genuine, deep and real characters ... The tension and suspense are in overdrive ... A series that is timeless!" — **In the Library Review**

Stand Alone Thrillers

Can't Stop Me
Your Son Is Alive
Long Lost
No More Lies
Blind Justice
Don't Leave Me
Final Witness
Framed
Last Call

Mallory Caine, Zombie-At-Law Series

You read that right. A new genre. Part John Grisham, part Raymond Chandler—it's just that the lawyer is dead. Mallory Caine, Zombie at Law, defends the creatures no other lawyer will touch...and longs to reclaim her real life.

Pay Me In Flesh
The Year of Eating Dangerously
I Ate The Sheriff

ABOUT THE AUTHOR

James Scott Bell is the multi-bestselling author of thrillers and books on the writing craft. He is a winner of both the International Thriller Writers Award and the Christy Award (Suspense). He attended the University of California, Santa Barbara, where he studied writing with Raymond Carver, and graduated with honors from USC Law School. He lives and writes in Los Angeles.

JamesScottBell.com
JamesScottBell.substack.com

Made in the USA
Las Vegas, NV
06 February 2025